GW01236771

David Jessop was born in Mansfield, England and studied Modern History at Queen Mary College, University of London. He also has a doctorate in History from Dalhousie University, Halifax, Canada. Most of his life was spent in Finance and Charity work in the UK and North America. *The Vicar of Abchurch* is his first novel.

For my wife Karen, who is a constant support; for Bo Wang whose encouragement kept me working on the manuscript; and for all church Clergy who are on duty 24/7.

David Jessop

THE VICAR OF ABCHURCH

AUSTIN MACAULEY PUBLISHERS™

LONDON • CAMBRIDGE • NEW YORK • SHARJAH

A CIP catalogue record for this title is available from the British Library.

ISBN 9781398448391 (Paperback)
ISBN 9781398448407 (Hardback)
ISBN 9781398448421 (ePub e-book)
ISBN 9781398448414 (Audiobook)

www.austinmacauley.com

First Published 2022
Austin Macauley Publishers Ltd®
1 Canada Square
Canary Wharf
London
E14 5AA

Chapter 1

January

Aubrey and his wife Joan, both wrapped up warmly against the biting cold, paused to watch. In front of them, a group of hardy tourists was impatiently stamping on the stone slabs set evenly in the small square, trying hard to listen and concentrate as their enthusiastic guide described the scene before them.

"Now before we finally go for that late pub lunch I keep promising you," the guide laughed, "just a few moments in front of this building on the north side of the square, the Church of St Mary Abchurch. Sorry, we can't get inside. As you can see, it's closed and barred. It's no use trying the door. It's always firmly locked no matter which day I bring a group to see it. A great pity, really, as it's one of Wren's finest City churches, built not many years after the Great London Fire of 1666.This brickwork outside, I'm afraid, really doesn't do it justice. The guide books tell us it is actually one of the very few churches that the famous architect Sir Christopher Wren would recognise as his own work, excluding St Paul's Cathedral, of course, if he were to come back today. As we have seen this morning, so many of the others have been altered or destroyed over the centuries. In my opinion, the

Victorians particularly have a lot to answer for! Never mind, as we can't get inside, you will have to buy my own modest guidebook to see the pictures." And he held up a thin paperback as if swearing on oath before judge and jury. "No one in England goes to church nowadays, of course. So what you can see if you ever do get inside is at present not really a church at all; nothing more than a decaying collection of ecclesiastical furniture, I understand. The Church of England files away its unwanted odds and ends in the place. Rather a sad note, I'm afraid, on which to end our tour of City of London churches. Now to the pub and over lunch, I'll see if you can guess what the name Abchurch means. You must all have thought the name St Mary Abchurch was such an odd title."

Aubrey, feeling rather angry at this description, made as if to speak to the guide but Joan indicated it was none of his business. Some of the tourists took photographs of the ancient brickwork and the diminutive leaden spire while others snapped 'selfies' on their smart phones as they stood laughing on the church steps, until at last they were all ready and off they marched, Christopher Wren and his amazing church architecture soon forgotten. The church, with its two high circular windows set far apart like widely spaced eyes, appeared to watch them sadly as they hurried coldly away into the January gloom.

Aubrey watched them leave, shrugged and removed his scarf, revealing a starched white clerical collar. "Well, no disguising the size of the task here," he said as much to himself as to his wife and, reaching into his coat pocket, he took out a small bunch of keys. He firmly gripped the metal handrail in front of him and climbed the few church steps leading to the main door. "I don't think we will bother with a 'selfie'," he laughed. "But let's see if when we get in, we at least can recognise the place as a church."

Joan, ever reluctant, followed him in, pretending not to notice the discarded drug syringes near the church steps.

The building they entered that January afternoon, St Mary Abchurch, is one of those places in the City of London which appear to have been forgotten by both religious and secular authorities, standing forlorn and unloved, away from the main thoroughfares on a small square between two alleyways. It has survived because its value, ancient ecclesiastical and therefore nationally protected, places it beyond the grasp of wealthy companies and property developers. And the City of London, not really appreciating the priceless jewel in its midst, passes quickly by in its eagerness to tear down everything old, in the name of progress and profit, and replace it with uniform boxes. The early twenty-first century so often seemed to value the run-of-the-mill and the commonplace designed on computer at architectural practice over the inspiration and hard work of ancient genius.

Yet, in truth, St Mary Abchurch doesn't appear to mind such neglect. Indeed, over her long life, she has learnt sometimes to relish the injustice of being undervalued and unloved. After all, as Aubrey and Joan had been told, it had suffered much worse. The bomb dropped on the White Hart Tavern at the corner of nearby Cannon Street in the autumn of 1940 shook her violently and took out her stained-glass windows with its blast damage. But she survived; a ready testament indeed to ancient building techniques. And on reflection, even that bomb might have been no great calamity to the church. Many after all had thought that Sir Christopher

Wren's spirit had never been reconciled to the nineteenth-century addition of stained-glass windows. And sympathetic restorers, sensing this, had been happy in peace time to replace fussy Victorian so-called improvements with copies of Wren's clear glass originals. Plain glass windows to let in God's pure light. So even the horrors of enemy bombing could be overcome and the church once again was able to purr in the sunshine. Parishioners and architects long since dead could now rest content.

After the war, the church was able to smile as before and lazily remember its glorious past. And it did indeed have a memorable history. Two hundred years ago, when abroad Lord Nelson was defeating the French, at home St Mary Abchurch had dominated this part of the City, it's small spire a beacon of Protestant conformity and order for the many small god-fearing houses which were pressed up close to it as if for protection. A large congregation then had been christened, married and buried within the sound of its bell. The vicar had administered to all without regard to wealth and status as was required of him in a parish paying allegiance, as Parliament had decided, to the English Church by Law Established. Rich Lord Mayors, after a lifetime of obvious giving, had left stone tablet record in that place; the desperately poor had left nothing and those too disgraced to enjoy the wedded comforts and certainties of conformity had secretly and sadly at night left their illegitimate babies on the stone steps of the Church; such baby foundlings being marked with the surname 'Abchurch' for posterity.

The Church had then been one of the centres of the City world, not unloved by it. Sea adventurers, empire builders, insurance men, stock brokers, East India Company merchants, money lenders and men associated with the African trade, many wearing powdered wigs, had come there to divine service on Sunday, willing to take risks in the week when on The Lord's Day they could be secure in the unchanging certainties provided by the twin pillars of the Church of England, The Book of Common Prayer and The King James Bible.

Then in Queen Victoria's reign had come the railways, which had rattled away the congregation. Suddenly, there were no longer men of commerce to come to Morning Prayer. The local houses vanished as large companies built temples to the new religions of profit and shareholder value. The empire became a place for administrators and soldiers not for risk takers and merchant adventurers. The East India Company was wound up and surrendered its position on nearby Leadenhall Street to fresh-faced ambitious young government men based faraway in Whitehall.

In the City, money men, commuting now from suburban villas, decided that there were too many churches and that such a structural abundance was impeding modern commerce. Few were left to argue with them and fight for Sir Christopher Wren's buildings. Their answer was to amalgamate parishes and pull down those churches which stood in the way of the new Victorian commercial realities. St Mary Abchurch trembled and kept very quiet, hidden away and dwarfed as she now was by large office blocks pressing in on all sides. But fortunately, the City of London forgot its gem and almost through indifference spared it. And St Mary Abchurch eventually found that she had won the territorial battle and she survived. Other Wren churches were less fortunate and were destroyed to be replaced eventually, as every modern visitor knows, by historic blue plaques.

But of course, as men of commerce in the City of London know only too well, survival is not one brief battle but rather a series of long campaigns, financial skirmishes which never end. Churchwardens and incumbents spent sleepless nights worrying when bills for repairs and running expenses couldn't be settled. City commercial livery companies tried to help, it is true, but so often other, bigger, more prominent churches laid claim to their largess. Few people attended Divine Service now, and visitors gave little money, convinced that the wealthy City of London must obviously look after its historic buildings. One tourist from the north country had been heard to remark, "Don't you dare give any money, my love. A church in the City of London! My God, the Church of England and the City Corporation, two of the richest institutions in the world! This place must be rolling in cash!" The churchwarden, overhearing, had smiled, knowing only too well that a so-called 'anonymous' secret monthly bequest from himself was all that kept the church from bankruptcy and the bishop's office quiet.

However, by the twenty-first century, something just had to be done. The problems could be ignored no longer. The bills still cascaded relentlessly into the church. Deep cracks were appearing in Wren's architecture, which had been designed before the underground train or the motor car regularly shook the building. Water inevitably found many ways to enter both the roof and the window seals, creating lasting damage, and the Church of England, already groaning under the weight of too many old buildings, no longer was willing or indeed able to underwrite churches which did not pay their way. St Mary Abchurch, now with no congregation, found herself facing a threat bigger than that posed by either Victorian developers or German bombs.

Aubrey stepped into the dark building and fumbled around the wall but couldn't find the light switches.

"John did warn me about lots of things here but he never mentioned the lights. There must be electricity, surely," he said. He took an old torch from his coat pocket and shone the yellow beam into the gloom. "Yes, I can see light brackets so there must be switches somewhere, but where?"

After several minutes spent bumping into tables, pew ends and bits of old carpet, he found the main switch board on the opposite wall and pressed several buttons. A few worked although most did not, but at least the couple could now see through the eerie light of a wintery afternoon. The scene before them was depressive; one of neglect layered with the dust and plaster of ages. Tables, desks, notice boards, discarded picture postcards and piles of newspapers filled most of the old pews. Broken light bulbs lay piled up in one corner. Electrical switches and plastic cable littered the stairs to a small gallery at one end.

Joan shuddered as her shoe stubbed a dead mouse. "That guide was right," she ventured. "This is not recognisable as a church. No, worse than that. It's a rubbish dump. No one has been here for years. And look at all these cigarette buts littered across the floor, in a church of all places. And, Aubrey, I wasn't going to mention this but did you see those drug syringes out there in the yard?"

"Well, church or not, John did assure me there was a regular Communion Service held here until quite recently,"

Aubrey replied irritably, wisely deciding to ignore the cigarettes and drugs.

"Maybe," frowned Joan. "But I for one wouldn't want to sit in all this cold choking dust, Communion or no Communion."

"This place needs to be loved," said Aubrey, who was by nature a kind man who refused to be cowed by Joan's premeditated distaste. "Loved and made attractive to the locals. I'm sure that will be our role. In fact, I know it will be."

"Your role maybe, not mine, Aubrey. You know my views. You're the vicar, not me," she snapped loudly and impatiently. "Don't get me on again about the Church of England. They saw a mug, someone who was not exactly a success. Didn't know what to do with him and dumped him in this God forsaken courtyard. You and this place can sink together but do not include me. Don't talk about 'our' role."

And defiantly, she turned up her coat collar against the damp January Abchurch cold.

The sneer in her voice hurt Aubrey but wisely, he decided to ignore it. By now, he had done a quick tour of the walls when suddenly, for a brief few seconds, a low watery sun picked a path through the January gloom. St Mary Abchurch appeared to awaken and sparkle. The dust seemed to vanish or at least not to be relevant. The old place appeared momentarily pleased and indeed relieved to see its new vicar. At that moment. Aubrey, a deeply Christian man, knew that he had come to an intended destination.

"But, dearest, just look at this place; forget the rubbish and the dust. Abchurch is welcoming us. It is reaching out to us. We can sort the dust, fix the heating, throw away the rubbish and clean the murky windows at the same time. But look! It's magnificent! It's square, like some of those Methodist chapels we used to see in Wales, and look at that carved wood behind the altar with its delicate fruit and flowers and the pelican there in its piety." His crescendoing voice echoed in the empty church. "And that painted dome! Just look at that ceiling! And the font with a cover on it! My goodness, darling, St Mary Abchurch is amazing. Come on, we talked for hours about this and you promised me we could give it a go."

Joan ignored him, produced a cheese and tomato sandwich from her bag and proceeded to have her own late lunch albeit not from a pub, defiantly standing up and still wearing her thick coat, the brief moment of winter sunshine now forgotten.

The tour guide had been right in one respect. Abchurch was indeed one of Christopher Wren's finest buildings. As the guide had said, its understated brick exterior gave no hint of the glories inside. The Victorians had tried to improve Wren's work with new pews, stained glass windows and other alterations, but had either been prevented from or decided against too much other damage, so the glorious work of Wren and his craftsmen was still visible on all sides. The small square box church supported on its walls an enormous painted dome which gave the overall impression of the space being extensive and airy. And the great carver Grinling Gibbons himself had made a large wooden reredos on the east wall with flowers so delicate that previous parishioners had felt they visibly moved with the motion of passing coaches in Abchurch Lane. The piece was at the apex of a wealth of other beautiful wooden carvings on font, pulpit and pews, and the wooden interior presented an overall domestic warmth to visitor and churchgoer alike.

The altar was really a small communion table which took its reformed Protestant place equally alongside lectern and pulpit rather than eclipsing them in the medieval Roman fashion. Sword rests where countless Lord Mayors had placed their weapons during visits, intricately carved poor boxes, a royal coat of arms, a figure of a pelican and several stone monuments fixed to the walls all added to the glory that was St Mary Abchurch. The building had been designed so that in the reformed tradition every member of the congregation could see and hear all that took place in any part of the interior. Wren had ensured that ministers could no longer safely mumble inaudibly whilst they performed archaic rituals hidden away from those in the pews. Nothing could be hidden in his St Mary's. The vicar of Abchurch would always be on show no matter where he chose to stand, kneel or sit. The congregation could see and participate in all services. And clear-glass windows ensured there were no dark corners.

"You know, dear," said Aubrey, "for me, it will be a labour of pure love to sort out this place. I almost feel that it was intended that we come here. Christ wants us to be in the City of London. Our last duty and mission for the Church. We can make a real difference to people's lives, you will see. I'm sure we can find a congregation from all these enormous office buildings, and do the Lord's work in this part of the City. In spite of what that guide was saying, those tourists just didn't understand what a real treasure we have here. The dust has not ruined Abchurch, it has merely preserved it for future generations."

Joan said nothing and grumpily finished eating her sandwich. She had said everything she was going to say on the subject over several weeks. She did not want to be there and could not hide her displeasure. Indeed, the cold weather only darkened her mood. She watched Aubrey as in his simple Christian faith, he fussed over pew doors, straightened the altar cloth, checked a few light bulbs, replaced a broken candle and collected discarded prayer books. But she couldn't help thinking that, a difference or not, as the culmination of a life spent in the service of 'The English Church by Law Established', being the Vicar of St Mary Abchurch was a meagre achievement with very little reward indeed.

Chapter 2

February

Friends both within and beyond the Church of England could not understand why Aubrey and Joan Braithwaite stayed together; except perhaps, as some imagined, through some old-fashioned clerical sense that marriage made before God was for life, and incumbents of all people should, therefore, set a good example and remain visibly in a relationship. The truth, however, was more prosaic. Aubrey and Joan came from generations of English men and women who have never contemplated dissolving their marriage. It was as simple as that. The matter never arose, was never discussed. In truth, it never occurred to them that such an idea was possible for themselves. Their parents were married for life as were their grandparents. Marriage by definition was ordained by God for your time on earth and you just got on with it without posing questions about personal happiness and such like. Constantly asking if you were happy was, after all, nothing more than a selfish indulgence of the twenty-first century. Life was a series of duties and obligations as well as of personal rights. The Braithwaites believed firmly that such duties kept society held together. And furthermore, the rise of the divorce rate was of great practical concern to Aubrey. During his ministry, he was increasingly called upon to counsel men, women and even children hurt by marriage failures.

In the early days of their married life, it is true and in the first rush of affection, Aubrey had felt that his marriage was blessed by heaven and rather pompously, he used to remind them both that holy matrimony signified the "mystical union that is betwixt Christ and his Church" as the Prayer Book wedding service would have it. Indeed, in the heady months just after their wedding, he occasionally chose this as the text for his sermon to the obvious discomfort of those divorced who were squirming below him in the pews. But such holy ideas had soon been forgotten, spirited away by the practicalities of life and the inevitable tensions the couple experienced trying to set up home in a tiny church flat.

And, anyway, Joan would retort that marriage was ordained first of all for the procreation of children according to that same Prayer Book. But no children appeared and eventually, as they both settled into a corpulent unloving middle age and moved from one parish to another, neither saw fit to mention the words of the marriage service again. Aubrey no longer remembered heaven's blessing; Joan just got on with the business of living and buried herself in domestic paraphernalia, choosing to forget children and if she were honest, sometimes her God as well.

Aubrey, a concerned, somewhat plain-thinking man, heaped his obvious gift for love and holiness on his parishioners rather than on his wife. He understood their problems, tried to help out with advice and sometimes a little money; although, of course, he never mentioned such profligacy to Joan. He prayed with them, counselled them and was convinced he was doing the right thing and making a difference. Aubrey had two rare gifts: the ability to listen without bringing all conversations around to the subject of himself and his own life, coupled with a firm reluctance to sit in judgement on anyone or on any situation. He knew that God had not given him the power of judgement. But he did understand that he had a real calling to exercise his priestly ministry and he was very happy and content in that knowledge, as are all those who are lucky enough to work in a profession which is also their main interest in life.

From an early age, Aubrey had known that he wanted to do something or be somebody in the Church, even though his parents were not, as was said locally, 'church people'. As an only child, he had become acquainted with the mysteries of Church life when as a young boy, he was dumped in the local parish mission, St Peter's, each Sunday. His principal friends inevitably, therefore, were members of the congregation.

The church would eventually take an even bigger role in his young life and even, indeed, in the lives of his mother and father. His parents suffered from bad health and in consequence, employment for them was spasmodic and occasionally the family had to rely on handouts of food and clothing, most of it coming from concerned parishioners in St Peter's. Aubrey himself was not able to go to university but had been fortunate enough as a young man to attend ecclesiastical courses at night school paid for by an elder of his church. St Peter's parish, therefore, became life's focus for the growing young man. He went through his own ministry as a consequence grateful for such kindnesses and, blessed by good health himself, he felt strongly that in his turn his role was to assist others as he himself had been helped.

Joan was of a more selfish and ambitious nature. She came from a family of senior clerics who were well-represented in Crockford's Church of England Clerical Directory. Her father had been a dean at one of England's prominent cathedrals and her grandfather had been a colonial bishop dispensing the gospel throughout vast tracts of Southern Africa. Brought up in a busy deanery and watching her father, she inevitably assumed the priesthood was there to fulfil ambition and that clerics worked tirelessly to scramble up the ecclesiastical ladder rather as employees in some giant heavenly inspired corporation. It never occurred to her that merely being a vicar could be ambition fulfilled.

February became a special month for both Joan and Aubrey. They had first met on a Sunday School February winter outing to the seaside. Aubrey's birthday was in February and Joan had treated him to fish and chips for the coach journey home. They would often laugh together about that day when the whole bus smelt of fish and no one would sit near them. And it was on St Valentine's Day, also of course in February, that they had first exchanged love cards with each other, albeit unsigned ones of course.

Later, when their relationship had become more serious, Joan had assured her father that Aubrey was obviously the ambitious type and worth marrying. He would become a bishop, a dean or an archdeacon at the very least. Her father and grandfather, quickly summing up the situation, had had other thoughts and had voiced them frequently in the past, especially when their courtship took on a more permanent aspect. Indeed, some of their words, lacking any element of Christian charity, occasionally came back to torment her.

"Look, my dear, Christian love is all very well as far as it goes and Aubrey does seem to relate to his parishioners," her father had said condescendingly one memorable weekend when visiting the couple during Aubrey's first curacy. "But I always feel God helps them who help themselves and I wonder can Aubrey manage upwards as well as downwards?"

Joan had stared. She had no idea what he was talking about so she had just let the matter drop.

Her father had continued. "Look, at the end of the day, you have to ask yourself will he provide for you properly? You are the daughter of a dean, after all. Will he be a real influence in the Church? Will he be the obvious candidate for preferment? Will he perhaps write a book or two? Will the rural dean regularly seek his advice? After a full life in the Church will he, as we used to say at theological college in Cambridge, have achieved a chauffeur-driven car?"

A chauffeur-driven car was a major status symbol for both father and grandfather. It defined the man. It made ambition and success obvious to all.

The neighbours noticed when it arrived and who got in and out. Her grandfather had not achieved this eminence and had never understood why colonial bishops were not afforded such a luxury when they came back home, a grievance which marred his rather long retirement.

Later, when her father had died, and sensing her own life was flashing by without obvious achievement, she had admonished Aubrey on one particularly dark, cold and soggy Sunday in February as he locked the church door after divine service.

"Daddy was a vicar in his early thirties, not just on a third curate's position. By forty, he was clearly going places. Look at us. It's pathetic, really!" she almost shouted as the rain poured down her back. "Who else do you know who has had three curacies? You run this parish while that lazy rector swans off to his place in France and you get little remuneration or even acknowledgement. I bet it's not raining in Nice! I don't compare our life to Susan's. She married well and Philip has been rather lucky in that bank. But we wouldn't even have our own house if my parents hadn't left us money. No money, no career, no children and it never stops raining!"

Aubrey locked the door and remained quiet. He was blamed now for the poor weather as well as for their lack of children and money. He did not reply. Such exchanges became more frequent and bitter as the years passed by. Lack of a family he could safely assign to God's greater celestial plan, but in truth, his dependence now on the legacy of his wife's family did irritate him, although without money himself, he had no choice but to listen. The money became Joan's trump card and rather as an ace, it was played regularly into every row, usually silencing debate whatever the topic under discussion.

For Joan, however, even though she liked talking of her legacy, money was not the real issue. Rather it was Aubrey's lack of ambition and desire for a serious career which irritated her because she knew what ambition could bring. He seemed so happy to spend time listening to the endless problems brought by a stream of parishioners rather than sending them quickly on their way, and passing valuable moments mixing instead with those who might help his preferment in the ministry. She understood now what 'managing upwards' meant!

Her father's house had been so different from Aubrey's. It had been witness to a regular assortment of politicians, industrialists, media people, well-known celebrities from the arts as well as senior clerics. Her own house instead saw an endless parade of the poor asking for money for food and clothing after carelessly using her spotless bathroom, and rough sleepers looking for a few coins to provide an occasional lodging for the night.

When she was growing up, her father had organised an annual festival in the cathedral grounds which attracted many people who were at the top of their profession on a national and indeed global stage. As a little girl, she had collected signatures from many of the famous and occasionally, she would bitterly take out the book, rather faded now, to recollect youthful rich times. The nightly television news sometimes chronicled the death of someone who had signed her book years before. And, of course, she had travelled everywhere in that posh car.

Nowadays, Aubrey expected her to go by the underground railway. In truth, travelling by tube had occasioned their first major row. For sometimes, on the train, men and women, to outward appearance respectable, seeing Aubrey's clerical collar would approach without inhibition to sit by him and tell him their problems and anxieties. Aubrey, always patient, listened and chatted amiably. He never turned anyone away. Until one day, a young businessman dressed in a smart suit had placed a cheese sandwich on his lap and said loudly to Aubrey in particular and the railway carriage in general, and in a sneering manner, "Come on, Jesus. Turn my cheese into fresh salmon. I'm bored with cheese for lunch."

Aubrey had merely smiled weakly. It was just one of those occasions which he had learned to shrug off. It was Joan, however, who was furious and still in the carriage, she had shouted at her husband as well as at the man and thrown the sandwich on to the floor. She had created quite a spectacle to the embarrassment of all. Aubrey had tried to pay for the sandwich but the man had hurried away. The horror of the incident stayed with them both for months afterwards. And indeed, from that time onward, she had made it clear that she would only travel with him on the underground railway if he first removed his clerical collar.

In her younger years, of course, Joan had just assumed that all existence in the Church of England was as played out daily in her father's deanery and it took a long time for her to appreciate the realities of the clerical life into which she had married. At forty, she had accepted that no children would be born. On her forty-fifth, birthday, thinking over her life, she had realised with a jolt that being a minor vicar was all Aubrey would ever achieve; indeed, all he wanted to achieve. At fifty, realising she must inevitably have slipped into the second half of her life, she had secretly sought informal marriage guidance from a counsellor used by her sister after Philip had admitted to a long-lasting affair with his secretary at the bank. But the counsellor had suggested that matters would progress if Aubrey came along also to their meetings. So she had just stopped going and continued busying herself instead with the unending routines of life.

There had even been talk of a mid-life romance – a strong word, romance – with one of Aubrey's churchwardens. Many in the congregation at an earlier parish had taken to sniggering behind their prayer books as the two exchanged words. But in truth, it really wasn't a romance in the accepted sense of the word. The churchwarden was lonely after the death of his wife and Joan liked the company. Nothing more. Aubrey had heard the sniggering, of course, as had many in the diocesan office and he was relieved when a kindly bishop had suggested a change of parish. St Mary Abchurch had appeared at just the right time.

Chapter 3

March

Aubrey was right. St Mary Abchurch was to be a labour of love. And for the rest of January, February and into March, as the days slowly lengthened he happily busied himself opening up the old building, polishing, sweeping and dusting it down. He cleared up the cigarette ends, called the council for its officials to collect the evidence of drug use and mended some of the wooden chairs. Joan agreed to have the large clear windows washed inside and out as his belated birthday present. And, indeed, even she had to acknowledge that the church did begin to sparkle when the early Spring sunlight really could get in.

Aubrey started work on an updated guide book and spent his spare time taking photographs to complement it. He fussed over the heating system, cleaned out the drains and threw away the rubbish collected during many decades. And in spite of her threat not to help, Joan did occasionally assist him and indeed strangely, if she were honest, she did start to enjoy the purpose Abchurch had suddenly brought into her life; although, she would never have admitted as much to her husband.

The issue for them both was where to find a congregation in the busy City of London which rushed around and through the square, apparently blindly, without even looking in. Aubrey assured Joan there was no need to worry. He was confident that Christ would always provide. And it was certainly true that by March, the act of just opening the church doors each day did encourage a few people to come inside. By the middle of the month, young office workers could be seen praying alone in one or other of the pews or just sitting to enjoy the peace. People popped in to admire the painted ceiling and the extensive wood carvings. Mothering Sunday was in March, of course, and Aubrey in anticipation bought a few cards decorated with maternal poems and flowers for visitors to take home. And he was pleased to see that this supply of cards was rapidly used up.

That month, a man came in and introduced himself as an electrician and offered to sort some of the wiring in the upstairs balcony which Aubrey had been too frightened to touch. The lights were soon working and when Aubrey asked him for his bill, the man refused all payment.

"No, God has been very good to me over my problem," he said mysteriously. "It's the least I can do in return."

During March too, an older man became a regular visitor and one day, he told Aubrey that actually he was Muslim but he thought God lived in St Mary Abchurch so he liked secretly to come there. He hoped the vicar didn't mind and, more importantly, wouldn't tell anyone. Aubrey had assured him that God was God as far as he was concerned and he wouldn't tell anyone about his visits and, indeed. he was very welcome to use the church as much and as often as he liked. The City guides, too, quickly realised that St Mary Abchurch was back on the scene and they now came into the church with their groups rather than standing outside, to show off its glories at first hand.

One day, an old lady in a wheelchair was brought in by her daughter. She said she had been married in the church at the end of the war more than sixty years before and in a flood of tears, she described the scene of her wedding day when Abchurch had been full of naval service men and women and the wooden reredos behind the altar, dismantled and hidden away against bombing, had been replaced by a massive Union Jack.

One Friday lunchtime, a choir of school children, smart in their dark blue regulation blazers, turned up and asked if they could perform an impromptu concert. They had hoped to sing in the cathedral but couldn't afford the entrance fees. Aubrey welcomed them warmly, provided crisps and pop and listened as the building cascaded with music and song. Many came in from the square outside to join them, sitting and listening to the music as they munched on their sandwiches.

Also, of course, as in his previous parishes, the new vicar found himself acting as an unpaid social worker. All clergy men and women in modern Britain anticipate this. Christ's ministers are so often seen as an unpaid arm of the social welfare department of central government, existing to deal with those cases of neglect dumped by secular authority in the 'too difficult' drawer. An agitated middle-aged man wandered in one day in March and asked if Rebecca was there. Aubrey, not knowing who Rebecca was, merely said not yet. The man now popped by most days just to be certain that she hadn't turned up and his contact with Aubrey appeared to bring him calm. Another man with a long ponytail regularly wandered in and handed out fruit drops and other sweets. Joan had been horrified and threw hers away but Aubrey just ate what he was given and said a few words of thanks and a prayer and offered encouragement. On another occasion, a woman of indeterminate age walked in and told the vicar her role was to help banish sin and luckily, she could do so in March as there was an 'r' in the month. Aubrey smiled, blessed her and thanked her for her consideration.

On Wednesdays, he began a lunchtime Communion Service and although at first, no one except a reluctant Joan turned up, eventually a tiny congregation started to attend week after week.

Aubrey was fortunate that the church organ was in good working order and on the day after he started the service, an organist, Bob, had appeared and asked if he could practice on the instrument. One thing had led to another and Bob had agreed to be the official organist of St Mary Abchurch for a tiny fee each month; money paid by Joan, of course. His playing, though rather strident, was very acceptable to Aubrey and he soon became as much a fixture in the area as the vicar himself. Joan had said he smelt of drink. Aubrey didn't pry. He was just pleased to get such a good organist for the church. And, indeed, it was after a comment from Bob that a hymn was added to the Wednesday service. One of the communicants offered to sponsor a hymn for £10 a week if they could sing something traditional from the church hymn book, *Hymns Ancient and Modern*, rather than anything recently composed.

"It's the lack of poetry and memorable biblical phrases as much as the repetitive tuneless din which puts me off a lot of modern stuff," he had opined. "You feel sometimes as if modern hymn writers have never read the bible at all."

Aubrey had readily agreed and when the music and words of 'Stand up, Stand up for Jesus' first echoed around St Mary Abchurch that March, even the very walls, recognising the melody, had seemed happy to join in.

As the weeks rolled on towards spring, St Mary's which had been ignored for years, now started to find itself, as in centuries previously, at the middle of the local area. Office workers, it is true, rather than householders as in the past began to talk about 'their' church and 'their' vicar. Aubrey had a small leaflet printed which described services and gave details of the church and his own availability. He handed these out and pushed them through company letter boxes throughout the local area. Joan said it was a waste of money but as the month wore on, office workers began to seek him out in return to talk about their anxieties or just to chat. In a real sense, the English Church by Law Established was starting to reassert its rightful place in the community. And older workers, coming from all over England, and happily remembering the habits of youth, regularly passed the time of day with the vicar and his wife, thereby encouraging younger men and women quickly to do the same. Aubrey and even Joan were often to be seen now chatting to some of the men and women in the square and even occasionally having a glass of sherry in one or other of the local pubs. Indeed, the manager of one hostelry, the nearby Vintry, even offered to put fresh spring flowers on the altar during the Easter break as a way of thanking the couple for just being there. The square in front of the church as well as being a place for ale drinkers now became an area where on fine days, people sat, chatted and listened as the organ cadences and chords of Bach, Handel and Mozart drifted high above them. And from this time, as even Joan noticed, drug dealers left the area completely.

During his long career in the Church of England, Aubrey had found himself being moved amongst parishes of widely differing ecclesiastical traditions, between what in the common parlance might be called high, low or broad church. He had no problem with this. Indeed, he had always felt that such diversity was one of the major strengths of the Established Church and he would wear whatever vestments were required. He had tried conscientiously to adapt himself to each change with the minimum of fuss until once, tripping over so many statues of saints and the Virgin Mary which competed for attention in the incensed gloom, and working for a rector who refused even to let women approach his vast cabinet of church vestments, he had realised with something of a shock that at heart, he was a Protestant who found such ornate trimmings quite distasteful and superstitious and he had vowed that if he ever found himself starting a church from scratch, an unlikely occurrence of course, he would go back to basics; he would create an inclusive church for all, one of faith with Bible, pulpit, plain altar and himself wearing only a pure white surplice.

And St Mary Abchurch now presented him with his chance. It was not a new benefice, of course, as the parish itself, if not the actual church, dated from medieval times. But now, there was no congregation to impose its views; no rich churchwardens to threaten withdrawal of funds if the vicar didn't fall into line. He could decide how his church was to be decorated and how the services were to be conducted. By Easter time, he was saying Morning and Evening Prayer each day as his appointment required and he had decided to use the Book of Common Prayer and The King James Bible rather than newer, more fashionable, albeit probably transient, forms of worship, to give the old place a continuity with its historic past. The poetic words and phrases of the sixteenth-century reformers, Cranmer, Coverdale and Tyndale once again reverberated around St Mary Abchurch and even people unfamiliar with these jewels of the English language quickly learned to understand and value them.

For the first three months of his new incumbency, Aubrey was left alone by the diocesan authorities. His church was not an immediate priority for the bishop and his team, weighed down as they were by rising costs and falling congregation numbers across the whole City of London. Occasionally, the area dean on one of his walks down Cannon Street looked in and said an encouraging word before quickly moving on. But that was all. By Easter, however, the authorities decided it was time to formalise the new arrangements at Abchurch; time to be clear on what was expected and more especially how the finances of the parish would be managed. Aubrey was, therefore, asked to come in to the cathedral offices for a chat. He had known this would happen, of course, and had secretly been dreading it. Eventually, he said he was available in the week after Easter.

"Don't take any nonsense from them, Aubrey," said Joan over breakfast when the appointed day came around, taking the kindly but firm tone she had learned in the deanery. "You are building a nice little congregation here and you might even start a Sunday service of Matins in May or June. Can you imagine, people coming here for Divine Service on a Sunday? Not that common in the City of London, is it, especially when so few people actually live here anymore. I wonder when St Mary Abchurch last hosted a regular service of Morning Prayer on Sunday?"

Aubrey readily agreed.

"But it's not about services, my dear. They will want to mention money, of course, and as you know I'm out of my depth with money matters. Remember my second curacy in Nottinghamshire when the Reverend Hodd demanded that I preach about money each Harvest Festival? I hated that. I still dream about those sermons! In fact, I hated them so much that I began to doubt I had a calling for this work at all. I vowed then that in my own church I would never mention money, let alone preach about it."

And it was true, money was just not referred to at St Mary Abchurch by anyone other than Joan, of course. But ironically in spite of this, the boxes and the collection plates were now beginning to receive regular amounts. In fact, Aubrey sometimes had to empty the boxes several times a day and his visits to Lloyds Bank on Threadneedle Street with the takings had become so frequent that he was on happy social terms with many of the tellers there. Local workers and visitors alike seemed to understand that the church needed money and by giving, they showed their appreciation for the lovely building and for all their new vicar was doing. It was as though even if in their busy lives many couldn't actually attend a service, an act of giving at least kept just a foot in the heavenly door.

Joan tried gently to encourage him. "Look, Aubrey, my grandfather used to say, it all comes down to money."

"Oh my dear, that's a bit harsh and calculating," Aubrey had interjected. "People have much more in their lives than money. And the senior clerics have a lot more than financial affairs to worry about as they go about the Lord's work."

"Well, that's as maybe," she had agreed doubtfully. "But I'm telling you, those parishes which pay their way get left alone, but the others," she grimaced, "Sheila over at St Botolph was almost crying the other day in Sainsbury's. I'll say no more." And she noisily cleared away the breakfast plates as a sign that the discussion was over.

Chapter 4
April

John and Adrian, two young clerics in the diocesan offices near St Paul's Cathedral, had been set the task of deciding what to do about the many minor parishes, including St Mary Abchurch, which are dotted throughout the City of London. Their work was part of a major new Anglican study on the future threats and opportunities associated with maintaining the Christian faith in the electronic and social media age. All options were to be considered; from amalgamating parishes, closing churches, selling them to secular businesses or offering them to other religious denominations. They might even become City museums. The two clerics were permitted and indeed spurred on to 'think out of the box' as modern marketing jargon has it. And at the end of their deliberations, they would be expected by the bishop to produce a robust report which would in its turn be acted upon by the ruling officials of the diocese rather than merely left to gather dust in the archives. The bishop had said he would personally receive their suggestions and he had encouraged them to believe that their own careers were being judged on the outcome. And as they both well understood, they would of course be indelibly linked to this final report for the rest of their church lives.

Both were responding with enthusiasm to the new authority invested in them and it seemed that they were clearly up to the task. Obviously enjoying their newly found prestige the two were already establishing a severe and somewhat frightening reputation amongst many of the smaller and financially weaker churches in the City. Joan's chat with the worried lady from St Botolph was merely one of several such conversations taking place throughout the Square Mile that spring which saw either John or Adrian making many surprise visits to several churches in the City of London.

On that morning in April, with Easter celebrations now over and recently back home, freshly invigorated by an overseas holiday, both were looking forward to seeing Aubrey. They had decided to call him in to the diocesan office rather than to go out to his church, an indication perhaps of just how unimportant St Mary Abchurch was on the list of parish churches they were studying but perhaps also an indication to any versed in ecclesiastical political matters that the fate of the place had already been decided.

"You have met Aubrey," said Adrian. "What's he like? His wife is a bit of a snob, isn't she? The daughter of some dean or archdeacon somewhere, with a taste for churchwardens if the rumours are to be believed." They both sniggered.

"Well, I don't know about that," said John. "I do know the bishop can be an old softie sometimes and I did think it strange that the pair got Abchurch. Not going to set the world alight, especially him as you will see. I just assumed he would be pensioned off and we could have then continued our confidential discussions about the property sale." He put his finger to his lips and winked conspiratorially.

"That building is such a derelict eyesore and such a drain on the profit and loss account. And no one has been seen near the place for years."

"I see," nodded Adrian. "Mind you, perhaps this new vicar is changing all that. I forgot to tell you that Leonard did say that the church always seems to be busy whenever he walks by it on his way to the cathedral. Not something you actually expect to see here in the City of London. His comments took me quite by surprise. Oh, by the way, I forgot to tell you, he heard the start of a service in Holy Week before Easter apparently," Adrian continued. "And he wondered what was going on. Then he realised the words being used were from the Book of Common Prayer. The Reverend Aubrey Braithwaite was using the 1662 Prayer Book. He was. I'm not joking. I'm being quite serious."

John rolled his eyes.

"To satisfy men's carnal lusts and appetites, like brute beasts that have no understanding," he sang in a mock chant from the Book of Common Prayer marriage service. "Well, at least that lot with their carnal lusts are a dying breed. The Book of Common Prayer! How many people have we driven away with that antiquated nonsense! We are in the twenty-first century, not the Middle Ages! The Thirty-Nine Articles were being recited as well, perhaps?"

"You mean the Thirty-Nine Steps."

They both roared with laughter as Adrian referred to a Hollywood film then popular rather than to the basic tenets of the Anglican faith.

There was a knock at the door and a secretary put her head around. "The Vicar of St Mary Abchurch is here," she said.

"Oh yes," said John as formally as possible. "Just give us two minutes then show him in, dear. Better bring coffee, cardboard cups will do, he's only a minor vicar, and no biscuits. We aren't having a long meeting."

Five minutes later, Aubrey, by now quite nervous, was escorted in. He had not slept well, rehearsing over and over again in his mind the positive things that had happened at St Mary Abchurch since that cold day in January when he and Joan had been given the church keys. As a prompt, on Joan's advice, he had listed a few positive points on a sheet of paper, which he now clutched firmly in his left hand. The list included everything from mention of the services, the new and growing congregations and the cleaning and general care of the building.

"Ah, Reverend Braithwaite," said John offering a brief limp hand. "Nice to see you again. This is my colleague, Father Adrian. Please take a seat."

Aubrey collapsed into the offered chair.

"Coffee OK? Sorry, we only have cardboard cups and no biscuits, but it's our austerity drive."

"I don't drink coffee," said Aubrey weakly. "But it's all right, I don't need a drink, thanks."

"Now," said John trying to sound both managerial and interested, "how is it going at Abchurch?"

His question was obviously rhetorical because as Aubrey looked down at his paper and started to reply, John continued, talking quickly and obviously trying to impress.

"Look, we are all busy people, Reverend Braithwaite. Adrian and I are working hard on a new diocesan plan to provide a future for City churches and I'm seeing the bishop at 10.30 to go over the details. St Mary Abchurch will be part of our scheme, of course, but first we wanted to see you to talk about the money we will require from St Mary's; the family purse, parish rate or whatever it's called nowadays."

He flourished his arm in the air, trying to appear mature and statesmanlike, older and wiser than indicated by his years.

"To cut to the chase, I'm instructed by the bishop to say that you can have St Mary Abchurch for let's say a couple of years or perhaps longer at a rate of, now let me see," he continued officiously as he moved papers around the table in front of him. "Ah yes, £25,000 a year. I know that sounds like a large figure but our expenses keep rising and without that, I'm afraid Abchurch has to close. Now I see also from the files that you are in your mid 60s so not far off 70 and official retirement, I think we touched on that briefly in January when you came to see me. Well, perhaps there might be the chance of early retirement, on a reduced pension, of course. I can't promise, but you never know, when we finally close, eh, I mean if we were to decide to close St Mary Abchurch."

He noisily and busily put his papers to one side and looked slyly across at Aubrey for a response. Aubrey sat and stared, looking from one to the other in shocked silence. He could hear the bracket clock ticking on the nearby Georgian sideboard. His mind was a blur. He felt hot. He couldn't think how to respond. The appropriate words just wouldn't form in his mind. He remembered the children singing so enthusiastically at lunch time and the dear lady who had been married in St Mary Abchurch in 1945 with all her life before her. The sum mentioned was impossible to collect, of course, on top of all the running expenses. Joan's grandfather had been right, life did just come down to money. Those who were good with it prospered; the others did not. He had assumed that the Church of England was different, that it stood back from this financial maelstrom. But it just didn't. He saw that now.

"Reverend Braithwaite, did you hear me? Do you understand what I'm saying?" asked John. "Perhaps I should have finished what I had intended to say. St Mary Abchurch along with most of the City parishes will take its part in our new ecclesiastical strategic planning process. Perhaps I didn't make that clear, it's not just about money. But can I tell the bishop that you are on board with the financial side of our new diocesan plan even though you obviously don't know the other details yet? We are calling it 'Faith For All' by the way, 'FFA'. The bishop himself thought up the initials. And St Mary Abchurch will obviously be included. The theme is making the modern church relevant to our busy lives by cutting away the dead wood, so to speak, accumulated over centuries. We will be asking the question as to whether we need parishes at all. But there's more to it than that, of course. The whole exercise, which Adrian and I are working on, will be overlaid with a partnership paradigm."

"A partnership what?" asked Aubrey meekly.

"A partnership paradigm. Look, I don't want to give you the details now," John continued. "I can't keep the bishop waiting. Let me just say that we have had a rather expensive American consultancy company helping us work on the project for several weeks and directors from New York are due to present their findings to us all next month. You must come along to the presentation and reception. We are having wine and nibbles and such like. I will see you get an official invitation, although I think you must be on the guest list already."

And he wrote a note to himself with a flourish on his pile of papers.

Aubrey must eventually have said something in reply; although, thinking about it later, he couldn't remember what, and he suddenly found himself, as if by magic, next door in the paved area in front of the cathedral by the statue of Queen Anne, surrounded by a noisy group of happy foreign tourists. His hands were trembling and he realised with a start that he had left his note somewhere.

Oh well, it hardly matters now, he thought, and disentangling himself from the chattering visitors who were now milling about the cathedral steps, he began to walk slowly back up Cannon Street.

"I've been doing this job for over forty years," he said to no one in particular. "And after all that time, it's only about money. I was on my second curacy before those two were born. Just think of that, Aubrey! And it felt like I was in the headmaster's study. I have never heard of paradigms. What a failure I am. Gosh, my friends at St Peter's would have been so embarrassed to have sponsored me into the Church if they could see me now."

He looked, without really seeing, at the clothes in the various shop windows and he spent an age staring at mobile phones arranged in one particularly extravagant display. An obliging shop assistant came out sensing a possible sale but Aubrey just mumbled something and hurried quickly on up the street.

Perhaps, I should have spent more time with the archdeacon or the bishop. Managed upwards as Joan keeps saying. he thought. *Just invented a reason to be around the diocesan office as Andrew does.* He thought of one of the local rising stars. *He's getting on well if the rumours are to be believed and promised senior preferment by all accounts and his church is usually empty. How he does it, is a mystery.* He stopped himself. "No, Aubrey, you can't change now and its unchristian to even think such things, let alone say them. Do forgive me, Lord."

He crossed over Cousin Lane and continued through the crowds past Cannon St station and on towards London Bridge when suddenly, two young ladies, both dressed in spring-like yellow, accosted him.

"Hello vicar, how very nice to see you," said one called Karen. "You look lost in thought. This is my friend, Nancy. She has just joined the bank and she will come to Communion today and every Wednesday."

Aubrey, always professional and caring, greeted them both and said how pleased he was to have another communicant and if she ever needed him, she only had to ask.

"Well, there you are, Nancy, what did I say," said Karen. "I told Nancy how much I enjoyed attending your church, Vicar, and I took the liberty of saying she could probably have her wedding here in the City if she played her cards right. This might be your first wedding in St Mary Abchurch, Reverend."

And all three laughed and chatted happily in the bright sunlight; the diocesan office and paradigms briefly forgotten.

Aubrey said his goodbyes and crossed over busy Cannon Street by the pedestrian crossing near Boots the Chemist. He glanced at the London Stone monument recently polished and re-erected on the north side of the thoroughfare and sauntered into Abchurch Lane and faced his church. The small stone square in front of him was quite busy even though it was barely eleven o'clock. Business men and women, precariously carrying coffees in paper mugs whilst texting on their mobile phones, criss-crossed the space, miraculously without running into each other or even spilling their coffee. Two men were delivering beer to the Vintry pub and they stopped for a brief word with the vicar. The manager of an investment bank around the corner was walking up and down, obviously trying in his mind to sort out a particularly difficult business problem. He nodded hello and continued his perambulation across the square.

The sun makes such a difference to the mood of the place, thought Aubrey. And he made a mental note to weave this idea into one of his sermons.

It was then that he noticed Joan. His wife, who also had not slept well, had spent the last two hours doing tasks which didn't really need doing. She had polished the church silver yet again, dusted the pews and fussed over sorting the files in the vestry office, anything indeed just to fill in the lengthy minutes until Aubrey returned. She had been standing on the church steps for what seemed like an age when she spotted her husband at the same time that he saw her. She looked at him across the square and she knew. She knew it was bad news. She knew what bad news looked like. As a girl, she had often watched church ministers leaving her father's study after a difficult interview. She could smell bad news. No one had to tell her. She just knew, she could read the runes all right!

Aubrey tried to deceive her but his figure all hunched up spoke the truth for him. Hurrying over, he forced himself to break into a smile.

"My goodness, my love, the diocesan offices are really splendid. Georgian furniture, I should imagine. And a lovely smell of polish," he said.

Joan just looked at him. "Well, was I right? All about money, was it?"

"Well yes, money was mentioned at the end of the meeting," Aubrey stammered. "But they also told me about some new major review and presentation that will include our parish. We are invited to attend its launch next month."

He couldn't actually remember if Joan was to be included in the invitation but he thought it a nice touch to say so anyway.

"And how much do they want?" Joan's attention was not to be diverted by talk of presentations or the smell of polish.

"Oh my dear, you do have this tendency to reduce everything to pounds and pence." He looked down at his shoes. "Well, I suppose something like £25,000 was mentioned," he finally admitted.

"£25,000, £25,000!" she almost shouted. "Over what period?"

"Well £25,000 a year, every year we are here."

Joan's face turned visibly purple. "Aubrey, this is some sort of joke," she spluttered. "I must still be asleep. £25,000 on top of our running expenses, I assume! The damn cheek of them!"

"Please don't swear, dear, and please keep your voice down, people are listening," said Aubrey glancing at two builders lounging on the bench near the church door who were obviously straining to listen.

"Swear, I'll give you swear! I can say much worse than that!" She was bellowing now. "You have worked day and night here opening up this derelict place. No, what am I saying, we have worked day and night. You, at least, get a stipend. I am the unpaid skivvy. Not so much as a thank you. £25,000, £25,000! Did they actually thank you for all your work, all our work, all the hours, all the cleaning? All the money I've laid out to clean those enormous windows and the like?" She looked menacingly at Aubrey.

"Well, not really, dear. I think they just want to shut the church and pension me off if I am honest."

"Oh yes, I'm damn sure they do. Get rid of you on a reduced pension just as you are in the final lap of your working life!"

Joan stormed back into the church. Aubrey followed meekly, inwardly thankful that the building was empty and that the workers outside couldn't hear now, and he decided it prudent not to remonstrate again about swear words.

Trying to change the subject, he said, "You know, my dear, I often feel that St Mary Abchurch is one of St Paul's lost children. I was thinking that this morning before the meeting, when I was in the midst of all those tourists on the Cathedral steps. So many of Sir Christopher Wren's church masterpieces, of all shapes and sizes, used to nestle close to their great father. The cathedral could see them all and even in the dark could hear them chime the hours, reassuring him that they were all well. Sunday morning must have been glorious as one bell after another rang out a welcome to London's parishioners and answered the great peal of the bells of St Paul's itself. I imagine him checking them off on his catalogue of saplings. You know, the Cathedral must have panicked when the Victorians culled his flock, and erected massive office blocks to obscure many of those remaining.

We know Abchurch is here but the Cathedral can't see her anymore and that must worry him. We must repair the old bell in the tower to let St Paul's know that his daughter is both alive and well."

Aubrey looked at his wife for a comment.

Joan just ignored such musings. She was not to be diverted now she was in full flow. She put up a hand to silence him.

"Oh do be quiet, Aubrey. I'm not in the mood to listen to one of your sermons. You know, I think it is fitting that we should be allowed a second interview with the bishop's office, perhaps even with the bishop himself. That's the least they can grant. A sort of ecclesiastical appeal. And I will go along with you this time."

Aubrey felt himself inwardly shudder.

"Leave it to me, my dear. I've worked in the Church of England long enough to understand how they think and work," he said.

"And I haven't?" exploded Joan, her face becoming more purple than before. "My father was a dean I remind you, Aubrey, a dean in a major cathedral. And my grandfather was an Anglican bishop in Africa. He organised and ran his province through many years of toil. Understand how they think and work," she repeated.

"Yes, dear," said the vicar. "Well, we'll see."

And with that, he rushed off to find a clean surplice in thankful preparation for the midday Communion Service.

Chapter 5

May

May that year was unseasonably warm and the leisurely lengthening days were enriched by the colourful annual display of plants and flowers to be found in the many squares, lanes and alleyways of the City. Those who are not used to London and are particularly ignorant of the Square Mile imagine it to be merely a concrete jungle dominated by traffic fumes, noisy lorries and impatient, rude commuters. Nothing could be so wrong. It is a place of rushing crowds to be sure, especially at peak hours. But at other times and away from the main streets in the back lanes, birds sing as they do in country areas and trees and flowers readily grow, encouraged by the gardeners of the City Corporation. Garden tubs, window boxes and cultivated forgotten churchyards can be found on all sides, adding to the rich colour of the civic scene. And the sunshine, of course, pours out the pub drinkers on to the pavements, drinkers who, themselves as commuters although often noisy, are seldom rude.

St Mary Abchurch luxuriated in this vernal abundance. Local workers brought flowers into the church, and inebriated bankers came inside and gave money as if to excuse and apologise for their liquid excess. The springtime brought an additional sense of community to Abchurch Square, and St Mary's, under Aubrey's seasoned guidance, provided a focal point to the whole area which was rather reminiscent of times long past. In this part of London, the Church of England once again was performing its role as an institution established by law for the use and spiritual nourishment of all.

May was the month the diocese had scheduled for its presentation to City of London clergy although in truth, the latter, worried now what the consultants might conclude, had no time to enjoy the flowers in their midst or to listen to birdsong. Clerical rumour and gossip reverberated in churches everywhere that month and most of it was very negative indeed. Everyone expected churches to be shut and parishes to be amalgamated. No one expected to hear a note of growth. Most clergy had a negative story to tell about a visit from John and Adrian as the two diocesan officials wandered around from church to church with notebooks and iPads in hand.

The one exception in this sea of concerned chatter, however, was St Mary Abchurch. Here, Aubrey was not gossiping; although, he couldn't help but hear the rumours, of course. Joan came back regularly from shopping trips with the latest story of doom. In truth, presentations had no fear for Aubrey. He was too old to bother much about them. He didn't really like them anyway. They took him away from the important day-to-day work of his ministry and the problems of his parishioners. Presentations with their clip boards, charts, overhead projectors and other modern paraphernalia were inevitably followed by a question-and-answer session and these he especially hated. He could never think of a question and he usually found himself shrinking in his seat in case the presenter picked upon him to say something.

Even worse than presentations, however, were overnight conferences and clergy retreats. His real dread was to receive an invitation to attend one of these. At such conferences, and they were becoming more frequent, it felt as though you were being imprisoned for days on end with no possibility of escape. At one such retreat entitled "Ministry and Mission", held in deepest rural Suffolk he had embarrassingly fallen asleep during one particular monotonous lecture, after a very late dinner the night before, and as a result, had been the butt of jokes for the rest of the week.

"Hope you aren't snoring when St Peter opens the Heavenly Gate," smirked his clerical neighbour to general laughter.

Aubrey had blinked, apologised and just tried to give a watery smile.

"That red wine last night finished me off," he had proffered as explanation and excuse.

Anyway, that May, he had decided to decline the offer to attend the presentation in the diocesan offices, claiming a fictitious previous engagement as an excuse. He had received his invitation letter, of course, as the Reverend John had promised, and had thought it over for several days before replying but eventually he had called the diocesan office to express his regrets. He was interested as St Mary Abchurch would inevitably be discussed and thinking about it afterwards, he realised he probably should have been present. But regrettably, on the morning of his disastrous interview in April, he had mentioned the invitation to Joan and he knew she would want to accompany him. She would probably use the occasion to harangue the bishop, the archdeacon and goodness knows how many other senior clerics about that £25,000. The presentation would merely give her a chance to reopen his previous meeting, except that this time, his problems rather than being contained in a small office would be broadcast to an enormous audience. The sheer horror of such an idea made him perspire. No, much safer for all if he just stayed away. After all, he told himself, these presentations usually had a political agenda around career development. Clerics would use them to impress the bishop and at his age, it was not as though he had a career to develop or a need to impress. And, anyway, Trinity started at the end of May that year and he always liked to compose particularly thoughtful sermons for his services then. The following sentence should be sermons not sermon. He would use the time to work on his sermon instead. And more importantly he could tell that Joan had obviously forgotten she was to be invited.

In the event, however, it was rather a shame that Aubrey and Joan didn't go, because the presentation, like many such expensive corporate arrangements, set to a formula and followed by wine and canapés, as well as covering possible church restructuring, did also give a glimpse of political manoeuvring within the diocese. In this, Aubrey was quite correct. That evening in May, the movements up the clerical ladder became obvious to all. And inevitably, St Mary Abchurch was also mentioned on the slides and over the nibbles and wine.

The consultants had worked on the project with John and Adrian for many months, visiting churches in the City of London and eventually parishes throughout England and Wales. Their travel budget was quite enormous. Indeed so thorough had been their analysis that the senior directors had felt the need to investigate Anglican practices in dioceses as far away as New Zealand, Australia and Canada. Their report, of course, had to be credible and to be credible, all possible options naturally had to be documented.

The result was the expected recommendation that some parish churches might be closed or even sold. But the bishop had insisted that this conclusion was not actually to be voiced so starkly that May evening. He was adamant on this point. The vicars personally affected had not yet been told and several non-clerical bodies such as the Georgian Society and the Victorian Society would also need to be consulted about the findings. And the bishop knew from long experience that such discussions could become heated and protracted. Then when this was all behind him, he would need to think carefully how to present the overall findings to the press in the best possible light. The wording of the press handout would be all important and would require careful construction jointly with the Archbishop of Canterbury's staff at Lambeth Palace. All this would take time and couldn't be rushed. This evening, the consultants could present their general thoughts without becoming too explicit. But he thought as far as possible, it still had to be an exercise in transparency and inclusion. Isn't that what they say nowadays?

The heart of the report pointed to an amalgamation of several parishes into webs of clerical control, rather in the way airlines set up hubs of power and influence. One or two ambitious young men had been lined up to give input to the consultants and if rumour was to be believed, had even been told what to say to them. John and Adrian in particular were clearly set to benefit and that May evening, they beamed as they welcomed the clerics, offered them drinks and gave out pens and notepads.

But it was the Reverend Andrew Grist who was having the most difficulty in controlling his excitement and anticipation over the Faith For All presentation that May evening. Wearing a new suit from Marks and Spencer and a freshly starched clerical collar, and clutching a hardback copy of the book *How to write a Marketing Plan*, he fussed excitedly around the gathering attendees. He smiled at everyone as they arrived, laughed in an exaggerated fashion when someone tried to make a joke, and while appearing to listen with interest to junior clerics standing around him, looked straight through them at the bishop and important decision makers grouped on the far side of the room, hoping, of course, to catch their eye. All in the room knew that Andrew would use the report to catapult his career rapidly forward. And when everyone was present and had taken a glass of wine and sat down in the conference room, it was indeed Andrew who introduced the proceedings that Thursday evening in May in church offices by the Cathedral in the City of London, whilst standing under a large poster proclaiming Faith For All (FFA).

In his smoothly modulated voice, he began by welcoming everyone, and, previously coached by the American consultants, he described in detail, complemented by glossy graphs and charts, the possible options for the ecclesiastical way ahead. His S.W.O.T. analysis outlined the strengths and weaknesses of the Established Church and the opportunities and threats posed by the situation in which it found itself, domiciled as it was in a city and indeed a country which had shaken off the habit of regular Christian religious observance.

He explained with a smile that the Church as an institution was still there even if its congregations were not and Faith For All – FFA – was to make it more relevant in the twenty-first century, put people back in the pews or at least persuade them to log on to the Church's website.

"Everything is a blank sheet of paper," he stood pointing at the screen. "We are getting back to first principle, and what it means to be the Church."

And he continued that he was not saying we didn't need all our church buildings but rather we need to look at how many we need and how we use them. He explained that for too long, 'church' had meant a building and a vicar serving a geographical area.

Seeing several attendees making copious notes, he said, "There is a hard copy of these slides for you all to take away when you leave, along with a little ecclesiastical gift." At the mention of a gift several in the audience, who were rather flush with the red wine, shook themselves wide awake and concentrated.

"Yes, we have a little model of the dome of St Paul's Cathedral which I hope you will all like, a sort of paperweight for your desk," Andrew beamed. "You will find them on the table at the back of the room as you leave."

There followed several slides, with graphs and colourful pie charts, many quite detailed which Andrew passed over very quickly so it was very difficult for individual vicars to work out what would happen to their particular church. The presentation rattled along until one slide was put up near the end of the proceedings which had a few churches listed with question marks by the side, and the astute observer would have seen St Mary Abchurch buried deeply at the foot of the screen.

One agitated cleric, who being teetotal had only had orange juice to drink not the red wine, saw to his horror that his church was on this list and with a question mark. He suddenly burst out, "Keep that slide on the screen. My church is there. Are you closing it? Is this a redundancy slide? We are doing such good work among the rough sleepers in our part of London. The bishop told me that no churches would be shut. I'm sure he did."

"Oh don't worry," Andrew reassured him, glancing at the bishop who looked agitated. "Inclusion here doesn't necessarily mean redundancy. We aren't looking just to close churches," he stretched the truth. "It doesn't necessarily mean closure if your building is on this list."

Others in the audience weren't quite so sure and feeling that Andrew was dissembling or trying to hide something, started to mumble. "So the rumours are true. This whole charade is a camouflage for shutting churches," said one incumbent.

Andrew felt himself perspiring down the back of his new suit.

"Well, perhaps, I can ask the archdeacon to comment to allay your concerns." He wiped his forehead quickly.

The consultants had warned him to ensure that this slide did not end up being the crux of the presentation and they had tried to coach him in that necessary marketing skill of passing on as rapidly as possible, without seeming to do so.

The archdeacon, older, considerably wiser and more skilled in presentations than was Andrew hastily stood up and moved to the front.

"Yes, perhaps, I ought to have said this at the beginning," he said calmly. "Andrew has made a wonderful presentation, as I'm sure you all agree, after many months of hard work whilst keeping his own parish going, I may add. Let me reiterate what Andrew said. Church redundancy is very much a last resort. After all, we do have control of some of the most historic and treasured buildings in the capital so we are hardly just going to dump them. No, today is really about reorganisation. As you will have gathered, I want Andrew now to put this report into effect, to have control of the main hub of parishes as mentioned on the slides. But in addition, perhaps more importantly, I want him to be overall incharge of the, how shall I put it, the challenging churches mentioned here."

And he pointed to the slide which was still on the screen.

"Let me repeat, this is not a redundancy slide in the accepted use of the word, redundancy. Take, for example, St Mary Abchurch," he continued, knowing full well that Aubrey was not there and that the other vicars barely knew where that church was and cared even less. "St Mary's will in future not actually be under the control of Andrew but will have what is called in the jargon I believe, a dotted line into him. Andrew will work closely with the vicar," he consulted his notes, "Aubrey Braithwaite, some of you will have met Aubrey, to see how that valuable piece of City property is maximised in the future. Forgive me," he hastily added, "I didn't mean to suggest that this plan was at all about money, but we do have to acknowledge that our churches are indeed expensive sites in their own right. Anyway, Aubrey and Andrew will work together to produce a parish plan, hopefully for presentation to a meeting such as this later on this year.

Then we will work on a project for each church in turn. Aubrey Braithwaite gets first shot at the FFA scheme, as it were. Such a shame he couldn't be here today," he repeated as he moved quickly on.

"Now we are near the end of the proceedings, I wanted to say a bit more about Andrew himself. Close your ears, Andrew," he laughed. "As you can all see, Andrew will be working very hard in the coming months to make FFA a reality, rather than just a set of slides; so, in fact, now is probably a good time to announce what some of you already know. The press office will put out a statement tomorrow saying Andrew will become area dean when Leonard retires after the summer break. We are promoting younger blood to a very senior position. It will be Andrew who as area dean is tasked with making FFA happen, building both on some of his own work and on the excellent effort put in by Reverend John and Father Adrian in drawing this plan together. In fact, a small appreciation from us all for John and Adrian might be in order at this point."

He clapped wildly to which a few in the audience followed somewhat half-heartedly.

The murmuring started again, however, and braver clerics put up their hands, so the archdeacon hastily continued, "Now, I know there are many points of detail which we haven't covered and many of you will have questions of substance on the plan so rather than covering further matters here, perhaps we can continue over the wine and nibbles in the other room. And when you leave, don't forget the church gift. Anything further, Andrew?"

Andrew came back to the front of the room and said, "Thank you, Archdeacon. Before we break up, I nearly forgot to say that FFA is really about us all working together. It is really about a partnership paradigm. We all have to buy in to the plan to make it a success. As clerics, we can only bring congregations back into our churches if we are seen to be a team. After all, we are all ministers of Christ here in the City of London. We must get out of the habit of thinking solely about our own individual parish responsibilities. Rather we are partners one with another. We should go to help our neighbours, as indeed the Bible tells us. And on this theme, as a way of finishing the presentation, why don't we now hug someone next to us? Not just a formal shake of the hand, mind you, but a proper warm hug."

Several in the room grimaced but tried to perform as required. The small number of female vicars suddenly found themselves in great demand.

A difficult presentation was finally concluded. And as most incumbents moved swiftly to the sideboard to refill their wine glasses, Father Adrian shouted, "Time for a group photograph. We will have one for everyone and another just with the senior clerics. Andrew, please stand in the front row."

Andrew Grist secretly dreaded these moments because although not a short man, he was not a particularly tall one, and he felt height gave authority. Tall clerics were always remembered. No one noticed short ones, or so he thought. Pressed amongst tall fellow clergymen in such photographs he had become adept at stretching on tiptoe to give himself both height and authority, and at the same time breathing in severely so as to appear fit and lean. Several pictures were needed to get everything just right. But at last, the photos were safely snapped.

The bishop, who had appeared slightly agitated earlier, now beamed and joined the retreat to the drinks and canapés; the archdeacon was already formatting in his head an announcement for social media; and Andrew breathed an audible sigh of relief.

It hadn't gone too badly. Good job he had invested in the suit, he thought. Pity about that redundancy slide. But he could assure the bishop that on the whole, much had been achieved this evening. It had been worth doing. Better to be transparent. Better to include people. It had not been a bad event at all. Certainly not as difficult as it might have been had Aubrey Braithwaite been present. That wife of his could be so awkward by all accounts. She might have even ruined the whole show! And everyone would have a gift to take away.

Then he remembered, there was the bill from the consultants which had arrived that morning. He must mention it to the bishop at the right time and get him to initial it. The bill was, truth to tell, rather greedy. In fact, he had never seen a financial figure written so large on any letter ever addressed to him before.

But, my goodness, this was the Church of England, not the Methodists or Baptists. The Roman Catholics would not have flinched at such a sum. And he could surely spread it over two financial years or perhaps more. He would need to discuss it with the church accountants, make them earn their inflated salaries for a change, he thought.

Out of the corner of his eye, he could see the bishop chatting amiably to two young curates in a corner of the room. Now he was obviously pleased with the evening and that's all that really mattered. Andrew felt he might safely enjoy a glass or two of Bordeaux wine.

"Area Dean," he whispered to himself under his breath. "Mother will be so so proud."

Chapter 6

June

As the days rolled on to the height of summer, the warm weather held firm. Rain had not been seen for many days and the City gardeners were kept busy regularly watering flower boxes to keep them in full bloom. St Mary Abchurch warmed herself in the midst of this colour and continued to assert her rightful place at the centre of affairs. A drinker outside the Vintry was heard to remark that only last year, no one really noticed the church but now, the church and vicar were full parts of the community, and it was difficult for most to remember a time when this was not so. Aubrey often came out to join the drinkers in the early evening and although he was always careful only to consume a small glass of cream sherry, his presence was appreciated by all. By now, he was on first name terms with many of them. Often, they would joke with him about some of the rituals of the church but as he remarked to Joan later, this was done not in a nasty way but usually in an informal manner of trying to understand more. The City workers, for the most part forgotten and ignored by the Established Church, were keen to understand why someone like Aubrey could be so happy and content when he was obviously not rich and had never actually ever even received an annual bonus. This was a mystery to everyone. Aubrey, of course, could take the ribbing and he was always ready to talk about the work and beliefs of the church.

That June, he persuaded two drinkers to have their babies christened at St Mary Abchurch and it was actually stimulating to talk to the people involved about the meaning of baptism and the commitment of god parents. Dusting off old registers and entering new names after a gap of decades was seen by Aubrey as the way his church, although apparently moribund, was suddenly springing back to life in that hot City June.

And it was certainly true that Abchurch now throbbed with new activity. Each day, many people came into the building to sit, think and often pray. Joan claimed they came to enjoy the cool calm away from the bustle and heat outside, rather than for thoughts of God. Aubrey didn't argue but agreed that this was probably part of the story, but only a part. There was more to it than that. They came in though, that was the important thing. When they had a need, they looked to their local church. And Abchurch was becoming so important now to so many people in that part of the City of London that the Vicar found he had to hold at first two then three Communion Services each week not one, as well as a Bible class and a shortened formal Evensong to catch City workers each Thursday before they rushed home through Cannon St and London Bridge Stations.

And Joan had been right when she had suggested that they should try a Sunday service of Matins. A hot June looked like the ideal time. The first one early in the month, the second Sunday after Trinity according to the Book of Common

Prayer, was poorly attended, just a few tourists and a couple of weekday drinkers from the Vintry. But by the end of the month, a congregation of up to forty people was obviously becoming a regular occurrence. Bob the organist put up a notice outside the church that month saying he was going to form a Sunday choir and was anyone interested. The response was very gratifying. The numbers were augmented, it was true, by singers from a nearby church who had suddenly walked out, disgruntled when a new rector unsympathetic to classical music traditions had been appointed. No one at Abchurch asked questions as to the motives of these singers; all were welcome and Sunday Choral Matins eventually became a fixture in the City of London that year, quickly appreciated for the richness and variety of its musical repertory and as well as, indeed, for the thoughtfulness of the vicar's sermons.

The City Police would often call in to see the vicar to check all was going well. Aubrey had always cultivated a good working relationship with the police and in previous parishes had held carol services for them and collected for police charities. They in return had always held Aubrey in high esteem and the same now was true in the City of London. They formed the habit of fetching Aubrey out if anyone was in serious trouble or even sometimes on the point of death. This did annoy Joan.

"Look, Aubrey, you are no longer a young man, this is an extra burden on you for which you don't get paid," she had complained one day as he searched for his prayer book to follow a concerned policeman. "There are Samaritans and other experts who look after people in distress and deal with these situations."

"But I am the Vicar of St Mary Abchurch," Aubrey had replied vehemently. "The Lord expects me to be there. That is my calling and I will go with the policeman." There was no more to be said. Joan became quiet and Aubrey hurried off.

Many, of course, wandered into the church timidly, not wanting to make a fuss, but at the same time obviously seeking help or advice, knowing perhaps that here they could talk in confidence, safely and without being judged. That June indeed an agitated, expensively dressed young woman came in, stared at the altar and carved reredos and seeing the vicar collecting prayer books after the lunch time service, just started to talk to him.

"You are so lucky, Minister," she said. "You believe in something; you actually believe God will listen if you pray, and, in fact, that there really is a God there to listen at all."

"My dear, that's very true," Aubrey had replied. "Don't you?"

"I would like to. Oh how I would like to." She had started to cry softly.

"Don't upset yourself," said Aubrey by now very concerned. "Sit here for a few minutes."

She sat down in one of the pews. And she continued, "Oh life can be so meaningless even if you're young, you know, especially in a place like London where no one cares. My father writes articles for the Guardian newspaper and he is always going on about how we live in a post-Christian society; how we have thrown off the religious superstitions of the past; how lucky we are not to be hide-bound by clerics and all their works."

She turned and looked at Aubrey, "But you know, I am not so sure. In spite of what he says, I'm not really certain that there isn't a God," she said.

Then she looked squarely at Aubrey and blurted out, "You have such a kind face with such caring eyes that I feel I could tell you anything. I stood at the back when you were taking a service the other lunchtime, and something you said was as though you were talking just to me. You know before my mother died, my brothers and I were taken to church every Sunday and I remember as a child sitting through the long sermons, reading that list at the back of the prayer book, which tells you who you cannot marry."

Aubrey laughed. "Ah, you mean the 'Table of Kindred and Affinity'. Well, I have to tell you, they have changed things so much now that I myself have to check who you can and cannot marry these days."

"Well," she continued. "I could never work out some of the people you are forbidden to marry and I used to say to my mother as we walked home, well, who would that be in our family? And she would say, 'Well, it means let's say you can't marry Philip or Reggie or whoever'. And we both would laugh out loud at such an idea as we held hands sauntering home over the fields. Then Mummy died and we just didn't go to church anymore. Daddy had never agreed with the church, you see."

Before Aubrey could reply, almost as an afterthought, she confided.

"My life is so empty. Oh I have friends, well, so-called friends especially on social media, and a good job. I make lots of money and I'm not ill or anything, but—"

And she stopped. Instinctively, she just took hold of Aubrey's hand and Aubrey in return held her hand between his.

"I just worry a bit that at the end of it all, there will be no place for me in the great scheme of things. Because actually, you know in spite of what Daddy says, I do believe there is such a scheme. I do believe in eternal life. And I do secretly try to pray occasionally."

"My dear," said Aubrey. "Christ will not erase your name from the book of eternal life. There really is no need to worry. Jesus came down on earth to assure us all of that."

At that moment, the Reverend Andrew Grist appeared at the back of the church, having come to introduce himself formally and following his presentation in May, to discuss the concept of dotted line responsibility and how they should proceed together working at St Mary Abchurch with FFA, Faith For All.

"Oh sorry," he said, seeing the two in deep conversation. "I can come back later. I was going to ring you to arrange a meeting but as I was walking down Cannon St, anyway, on my way to the cathedral, I thought I would pop my head around the door. But I can see you are busy."

Recognising Andrew, Aubrey excused himself from the young lady, and got up quickly to say hello.

"Well, I'm here every day so please tell me when would suit you for a chat, Andrew," he said.

And he walked over to the vestry to fetch his diary. They fixed a time to meet in early July and after a few further pleasantries, the Reverend Andrew Grist continued on his way up Cannon Street. Aubrey quickly looked around for the young lady but she was nowhere about. She had silently let herself out of the church. Concerned, he hurried over to the church steps to look into the square but the large mass of drinkers blocked his view and she had vanished. He returned to the vestry crestfallen.

That same month, a young man asked if he could sell coffee from a stall in the yard outside the church. Coffee shops could be so expensive and their coffee was of such indifferent taste, he claimed that he and his girlfriend felt they could make a worthwhile business and perhaps even encourage clients to look around the church. Aubrey was not so sure about this last point but he would always encourage enterprising young people and a monthly rent was soon agreed and storage facilities provided for the man's coffee cart in the kitchen at the back of the building. And as good as his word, the man did encourage people to look around the church and he was ever helpful carrying shopping for Joan or often shutting up the church for Aubrey. That month, he rapidly became one of Aubrey's Abchurch family.

In June, Aubrey noticed too that a change was coming over his wife. By the end of the month, although she did not commute into the City every day as he did, she sometimes arrived with him or came in the afternoon so they could go home together. Aubrey put it down to the sunshine and said nothing. Joan now would fetch polish and other cleaning materials from Sainsbury's in Cannon St. She talked about the church to the shop assistants there and to those working in Lloyds Bank in Threadneedle Street when she helped deposit the takings from the collection. It was as though St Mary Abchurch had actually given her a purpose and a renewed enjoyment of life. She still was critical of Aubrey's lack of ambition and fighting spirit and would occasionally say so loudly, but the charm of the place was obviously doing its work on her. And by June, she would usually attend most, if not all, of Aubrey's services.

That month, a class of American architectural students from Connecticut turned up, explained that they had no money, but wanted to make sketches of some of the best features of the building. Aubrey told them that he had no interest in money. There was no entrance fee, and they were welcome to draw there as often as they liked. For several hours, thirty or forty young people took over Abchurch, spread themselves over aisles and pews, and giggled and chatted as they made drawings of the pulpit, the font, the sword rests, the painted ceiling, the reredos, the royal coat of arms and the major monuments fixed to the walls.

"We have never been able to get into this church in other years," one young lady from the group explained to the vicar as he peered at her sketches. "We did try to get the key once but it wouldn't work in the lock. Too rusty, I think. And," she continued breathlessly as she sketched, "one church over the other side of the cathedral, believe it or not, wouldn't let us go in unless we each paid an entrance fee. Can you imagine! An entrance fee! We just couldn't afford it. I sent an email to tell my father about it, and he just wouldn't believe me that in Great Britain, in the twenty-first century, God was now charging people to enter his church. He said it couldn't be so and he told me not to tell lies about such a place as a church. But I said it was true and he said churches in London must be booming if they have to regulate traffic flow by charging entrance fees. And he wondered how the poor ever got inside. But you know I'm not telling lies. I was being very truthful. They wanted money, a lot of money."

Aubrey listened sympathetically.

"I can only apologise, my dear," he said. "These old places are very expensive to upkeep but I do agree with you. After all, we are not a cinema or theatre. No money changing in the temples here! While I am the Vicar of Abchurch, you can come as often as you like and there will never be a charge."

Joan, who was just returning from an expedition to the new shopping arcade near the Cathedral, overheard Aubrey's comments and later took issue with him.

"I listened to what you told those students and it is all very well to ignore things financial but the reality is that we here have to find £25,000 this year and every year. And where does that come from? You might ignore money, but the rest of us have to think about it. I agree that people are being very generous to us in the collections and donation boxes – that woman who slips £50 into the box every Monday is more than generous – as are the many City Guides who encourage people to donate. But the reality is that we are not going to come close to £25,000 and keep the lights on and the heat working in the wintertime. Every time I go to the bank, I can't help seeing that plaque on the side wall in Threadneedle St. You know the one I mean that says it used to be the site of St Martin Outwich until 1874. That church probably couldn't pay its way also and now it's a branch of Lloyd's Bank."

"Well, yes perhaps you are right," Aubrey murmured as he cleared up after the students had left. "But you know, I like to wonder what Christ would want us to do."

"Christ won't have to pay the damn bills!" she exclaimed crossly.

"I wouldn't be so sure of that, my dear. Stranger things have happened."

And he proceeded to bring inside the large blue 'Church Open' sign from its position at the top of the steps and lock the main door, wisely deciding to pretend he hadn't heard the swear word.

Chapter 7
July

The heatwave continued well into July. For the first part of the month, Aubrey worked in the church alone without the company of his wife as Joan, a tennis lover, liked to queue at Wimbledon for a ticket for the British Open or failing that, to watch the tennis tournament on the television. Having no interest in tennis himself, he secretly quite enjoyed this period of the year, when his wife failed to look over his shoulder with suggestions and criticism. This July, though, turned out to be a rather stressful month and anything but enjoyable at St Mary Abchurch.

Early in the month, the Reverend Andrew Grist turned up as planned to tell Aubrey about his new role as area dean and to explain that with dotted line responsibilities, he would now be taking a more direct interest in the management of St Mary Abchurch as he had been charged by the bishop with making a reality of Faith For All. He had come today to develop the concept that working together they could put in place a parish plan to bring more communicants into St Mary's. And with this in mind, he had brought along a hard copy of his slides from the May presentation and the model of the dome of St Paul's Cathedral, this one unfortunately broken on one side.

"I'm sorry," he said. "I'm afraid you didn't come to my talk and we only had enough models to go around. You have got the last one and it is slightly chipped. Take it for now, anyway, and I will remember to order you a new one."

Aubrey thanked him, put the dome on his desk and listened politely.

"Before we start on all this detail, Reverend Braithwaite —" Andrew began.

"Oh do call me Aubrey, everyone does," the vicar interjected.

"Well, Aubrey I have to say that I was somewhat taken aback when I came to see you the other day, at what you were doing. Although, to be fair, my visit was unannounced, it is true."

Taken aback, "At what I was doing? Why?" exclaimed Aubrey quite concerned.

"Well, it was a shock to see that you were holding hands with a member of the public, a female member of the public."

"What?" said Aubrey sensing his face was becoming redder and redder. "What are you saying? Holding hands with a female member of the public. Who was that?"

"I really don't know. It's not my business but some girl seemed to be crying over you."

Aubrey stared, trying desperately to think calmly. Then he remembered the smartly dressed young woman who had started to sob when they were discussing religious belief.

"Oh, that young lady. Well, she was in some sort of distress and I sat with her and tried to help. That was all," said Aubrey. "In fact, now I think about it, it was she who held my hand. I was listening to her concerns. I do a lot of listening in my ministry here."

"My goodness, Aubrey, don't you read the newspapers, or watch television? In the priesthood, we have to be so careful these days. Every week, it seems, there is a story of a clergyman acting improperly with children. The newspapers seems to thrive on such pieces," said Andrew.

"But she wasn't a child. She was an adult who needed help and who wanted to chat. In fact, talking of newspapers, I remember she said that her father wrote for the Guardian," replied Aubrey as an afterthought.

"Exactly!" said Andrew. "You are making my point for me. The clergy have to be so careful. You might consider taking one of the diocesan courses on dealing with the general public in the twenty-first century. It's never too late to learn, you know, even at your point in your personal ministry!" And he tapped a note to himself on his new iPad. He continued, "You are never going to get people to trust you as a priest or persuade the general public to use this place for worship unless you really understand how to interact with them in a modern paradigm."

"A modern what?" blurted Aubrey, now quite flushed and upset. "Since I started in this parish, everyone seems to talk to me about paradigms and if I am honest, I just don't really understand what they mean."

"Look, Reverend Braithwaite." Andrew had now reverted angrily to the formal address. "What I am saying is that this church building will never be used, never have a congregation unless the people are really sure about you as a priest; sure that you are a fully paid-up member of what I might call the modern world. And frankly, the first rule of that world is that you should never touch anyone, anyone at all. Not even, I might add, if they are dying."

"Not even if they are dying?" questioned Aubrey.

"Especially not when they are dying. Whatever would the relatives gathered around the bed think? You can shake hands when we 'Pass the Peace' at a formal Eucharist as I do in my church. Certainly, that is allowed and even encouraged but no more."

Andrew Grist was referring to a modern Christian practice subsumed into some Anglican churches in which parishioners are encouraged to shake hands individually with those sitting close by, and indeed sometimes to wander all over the church to find hands to clutch. Aubrey fell silent. He decided not to point out that the older members who attended St Mary Abchurch were grateful they were not required to do anything so un-British as 'Passing the Peace'. In fact, one old lady at his new Sunday Matins Service had made her views known to others in the congregation very loudly early in June on that very issue.

"Vicar, if you were to start doing that peace stuff," she had exclaimed in a menacing tone at the end of the service, "then I'm off. If Cranmer had felt it important to 'Pass the Peace', he would have included it in the rubric. And I think I speak for many others."

She was referring, of course, to Thomas Cranmer, the famous Protestant Archbishop of Canterbury who had helped pen the prayer book during the Reformation in the sixteenth century. Aubrey had winced and explained that there was no need to worry. He would always take his guidance from Cranmer's Book of Common Prayer.

He said to Andrew, "But my wife, Joan, informs me that rumour says you were hugging priests at your meeting in the diocesan offices in May."

"Well, yes, hugging priests is allowed, even encouraged. But there is a big difference between hugging a priest in brotherly love as part of our ministry and getting physically intimate with the general public. Surely you see that."

Both men were now clearly very upset and neither was listening to the other.

"You know, Reverend Braithwaite, I'm not sure we can really progress today with even the basics of FFA if you haven't been on one of our personnel management and interaction courses. Have you actually attended the basic 'Ministry and Mission' lectures during your priesthood? Did they have them when you were ordained? Frankly, from what you have said, one may even wonder if you should be a clergyman at all," he continued pompously. "However have you slipped through the net? A clergyman is a modern manager of funds and staff, and the message of Christ is our basic product which we need to sell efficiently and systematically. Surely you know that. We are general retailers such as you see on any high street. Do the staff at Selfridges or Harrods or other London department stores hold our hands and generally touch us? Oh my goodness, you really should have come to our presentation in the diocesan offices. I had wanted to talk today about how the two of us should interact in a new paradigm and how we would work to try and get a congregation to attend services at St Mary Abchurch. Even you must know this place is something of an ecclesiastical graveyard used by no one. Wouldn't you like to hold proper services here with sizeable congregations and to be a respected and trusted member of the neighbourhood?"

Aubrey looked at him bewildered and in disbelief. In reply, he began to stammer something about not seeing Christ as part of the retail trade but couldn't find the words so he just fell silent.

At that moment, they were suddenly interrupted by a policeman, flustered and very hot in the face. He had obviously been running some distance.

"Oh vicar, I'm so pleased to find you in. We are having some trouble with an American tourist who has collapsed in this heat on King William Street. She doesn't look very good at all. An ambulance is on its way but she keeps asking to see a clergyman. Do please come along with me, if at all possible."

Then seeing Andrew and sensing him to be the senior man, he said, "If it's not convenient vicar, perhaps your colleague would help."

"Oh, eh, I think the Reverend Braithwaite is the appropriate person," said Andrew somewhat alarmed at the thought of helping someone in the street. "Here, take this prayer book," he motioned to Aubrey.

Picking one up from the table, he handed it to the vicar.

"We can continue our discussion another day."

Aubrey took the proffered book and he and the policeman ran quickly out of the church, past the drinkers and coffee seller in the churchyard and left into Abchurch Lane towards King William Street.

Left alone in the church, Andrew picked up his bag and iPad and followed them also into the square but instead of turning left, he turned right, making his way into Cannon Street and on to the Cathedral. He arrived there a few minutes later and crossed over to the diocesan offices where he immediately ran into John and Adrian who were just coming back from an extended lunch.

"Am I glad to see you two," he exclaimed wiping his forehead. "People normal in this very mad world!"

"My goodness whatever has happened, Area Dean?" said Adrian. "Would you like a cup of tea?" And he indicated to the secretary to bring tea and biscuits. "The nice china, dear, for the area dean," he whispered.

"Well," continued Andrew, "I just went to see Aubrey Braithwaite to start talking about FFA. You remember the archdeacon said I should begin the process with a parish plan for Abchurch? Well, I took him the model of the dome of St Paul's. I must say he didn't particularly like it but there we are. But that man has so upset me. In fact, thinking about it, I'm not sure we should include St Mary Abchurch in our final plans while he is around."

Adrian rolled his eyes and laughed.

"Well, it's all very well laughing," continued Andrew angrily. "But I'm very upset. Have you met the man? He's a nightmare. It is impossible to reason with him. Do you know, he hasn't even been on a church personnel or marketing course? Did they do 'Mission and Ministry' when he was being ordained, I wonder? He hasn't the first idea how to sell to the general public. He is obviously a total disaster. I got away early because he had to attend some emergency in the street. Goodness only knows why the City Police bother with him. I'm surprised they get any sense. And you won't believe this but before he left, I handed him one of his prayer books and it was—"

"Yes, we know," interrupted John. "The Book of Common Prayer. Cranmer's Book of Common Prayer."

"Yes, the Book of Common Prayer!" Andrew almost exploded. "That antiquated dinosaur."

"Remember, Andrew, the bishop likes the old prayer book. Or says he does," cautioned John.

"Well, that's as maybe and, of course, I'm not criticising our dear bishop," Andrew quickly reassured them. "But my goodness, it sums up St Mary Abchurch. A no-hope place with a no-hope vicar from the Dark Ages. A disaster which can't be allowed to go on. Forget FFA there and forget marketing the message of Christ. I'm so cross about the whole place."

"Don't fret, Andrew. Abchurch and Aubrey aren't the future," whispered John conspiratorially. "Aubrey will soon be at retirement age, and very confidentially I can tell you that the bishop will let him retire early if we give the nod. Just drink your tea."

"Well, that's a relief," said Andrew wiping his brow. "A real relief."

"And," John continued looking slyly at Adrian. "We have set the parish rate at £25,000 for St Mary Abchurch. And that's £25,000 a year, each year. We got the bishop to sign off on the amount."

All three laughed and Andrew felt himself relaxing as he drank his warm tea. "No chance Aubrey is going to find that sort of money," he said.

"No," said John. "Of course, not. He will be down here explaining how we set him an impossible task. Then we will close the building and he and his wife can go and stare at the sea in some clergy graveyard in deepest Kent or whatever those sort of people do in retirement. St Mary Abchurch can then be forgotten. You have so much else to work on, Andrew, in the FFA scheme. Very silly you should be side-tracked by the Reverend Braithwaite. Our real problem though is the actual building. It is one of Sir Christopher Wren's best churches apparently, although I don't know it myself. People say it's quite amazing inside."

"Oh, I haven't really had the time to study it," shrugged Andrew.

"Well, take my word for it, Andrew; apparently, it is lovely. It would be a problem to knock down the building. All sorts of architectural and historical groups will become vocal. Even the BBC probably. But that area of the City is worth a fortune. It's a goldmine. Adrian and I are working very secretly on plans to use parts of the building for temporal use. A building company is prepared to buy it and preserve some of the best Wren bits behind glass while they construct an office complex around and above it. It will all be contained in something like an enormous glass bubble. A new Crystal Palace. But please say nothing, Andrew. The plans are really adventurous and farsighted. And such a scheme while of course bringing money to the Church of England would still have a religious aspect. We have insisted on that. Why we might even have a service of Evensong in the new complex a couple of times a year. There is much to think about with St Mary Abchurch. It will get sorted over the next 12 months we reckon, don't we, Adrian?"

"Oh yes, this time next year, you won't know the place," agreed Adrian. "But we have to be so careful with the media. If they get even a hint."

"Oh, don't worry," said Andrew, thankfully gulping down the warm tea, "I can be as silent as the grave when I have to be. These Rich Tea biscuits are going down a treat," he added as an afterthought.

Back at St Mary Abchurch, the situation also was calming down. Aubrey had returned from talking to the old lady who had collapsed in the street. When he reached the church, he was relieved to see that Andrew had left but he was surprised to see Joan.

"My goodness, my dear, I didn't expect to see you while any tennis was being played," he laughed.

"Well, I queued for ages. Then they said there were no tickets left for the show courts. And well, I'm getting just too old to queue and stand up, if I'm honest. I was hot and bothered and I suddenly needed a toilet. So I gave up and came back to the City. Anything happening?" asked Joan.

Aubrey told her about Andrew's visit and about the old lady who had collapsed in the heat.

"Actually that poor woman was in some distress. She must be well into her 80s and I don't think she knows anyone in London. She told me her name was Olive and that she had always hated it and that she just enjoyed amusing herself poking around the City streets, so her husband had stayed at home in Arizona or Arkansas or some such place. She kept smiling, looking at me and just wanted to hold my hand."

As he spoke, Aubrey shuddered, remembering Andrew's comments.

"So I made her comfortable on the pavement and we just chatted and I smiled a lot and said a few prayers. Cranmer's words are so often appropriate. I just gossiped. I told her about our life in St Mary Abchurch and how the area had suddenly taken on a Christian charm of its own, at least in my imagination. The ambulance seemed to take for ages. People were stepping over us and around us. The policemen, of course, were very helpful as they always are. Sometimes, I wasn't really sure if she was aware that I was there but thinking about it, I feel she did appreciate the attention. Funny thing though, at one point she did become very clear and insisted that I carefully repeat my name and the name of my church and she pleaded that I would go to the hospital tonight to check on her. She didn't want to be totally alone in a big place like London. So I said I would go along later this evening. Then at last the ambulance did arrive and, Joan, as they were carrying her inside she looked straight at me with her lovely clear blue eyes and said, 'The Book of Common Prayer talks about "overcoming the sharpness of death". Well, I've overcome it by not dying alone, but with one of Jesus's angels, even far away from home here in the City of London.' I said, 'My dear, you will be all right. You are probably dehydrated in this scorching heat. And I'm no angel, ask my wife.' And we both laughed. She blew me a kiss and as the ambulance door was closing, she asked if she could keep my prayer book and she told me to write my name in it and the full name and details of our church. So I instinctively did just as she requested."

Joan was standing in the vestry quietly listening.

"And will you go to Barts hospital this evening," she said.

"Yes, of course. It's not too much out of my way. Afterwards, I can get the underground home from St Paul's rather than Bank station. I do fear the worse though, if I am honest, because she was clearly near the end in spite of what I said in encouragement." And he stopped and wiped a tear from his eye.

"I will come with you," said Joan suddenly.

"Really?" said Aubrey.

"Well, I've never met anyone from Arkansas." Joan looked at him.

Aubrey smiled. "Oh Joan, I would really like that," he said and he squeezed her hand. "I do appreciate you saying that. I know you don't like going into hospitals."

"Well, probably best that you are not alone," she said. "And I think you should wear your clerical collar just this once on the underground."

By seven o'clock, the last of the visitors had left Abchurch and Aubrey and Joan locked the church door and pushed their way good-naturedly between the pressed ranks of drinkers standing outside the Vintry. Many wanted to chat.

"Two glasses of cream sherry for Mr and Mrs Vicar," said someone. "See we know what you like, Vicar, sherry, sweet not dry."

"Thank you but it's got to be another night," Aubrey laughed. "We've still got work to do."

The couple made further excuses and hurried down Sherborne Lane, into King William Street and along to the main Bank intersection. They continued on past the Mansion House, home to the Lord Mayor, then up Poultry and Cheapside, swept along by the last of the commuters towards St Paul's Cathedral. Rather out of breath by now, they followed the pavement around the corner and eventually reached the Old Bailey, turned right by St Sepulchre's church and into the gates of St Bartholomew's hospital, known to all Londoners as Barts.

"Good evening, Padre," said a harassed young woman on the main desk, seeing his clerical collar. "Can you find your own way or do you need directions? I'm on my own so I can't really take you to the wards myself."

Aubrey explained his quest and said that in the rush of the earlier occasion, he only knew the person he needed to see was called Olive, an old American lady. He didn't have any other details. The young woman typed the name Olive into her computer.

"Oh yes, here we are," she said. Then on reading the screen further, her tone suddenly changed from friendship to one of business.

"Well, I suppose you are her religious adviser and it's all right if I tell you the details," she continued to no one in particular. "I'm afraid to have to tell you that the lady you mentioned died earlier this evening, about an hour after she was brought in."

And then scrolling down the screen, she said, "Are you Reverend Aubrey Braithwaite by any chance?"

Aubrey explained that he was and that he had promised to pop by this evening – too late regrettably.

"Well, there is a note here from the duty nurse, asking to see you when you come in. Please take a seat over there and I will get this sorted."

Later that same evening, as Aubrey prepared for bed, he could hear Joan downstairs talking on the telephone to her sister, Susan. He smiled to himself as he undressed.

Joan does dramatise, he thought.

"Yes, Susan, it was so extraordinary," she was saying. "At the hospital, we waited for ages then a nurse appeared and returned Aubrey's prayer book which the American lady in King William Street had taken, and inside, the lady, who is called Olive, and is from Arkansas, had asked the nurse to write a few sentences. And she had written. Just a minute, let me get the book," she continued, "and I can tell you exactly…

Well, in the inside cover next to the stamp that says Property of St Mary Abchurch," she continued, "the nurse had written in a very tiny neat hand, 'Dictated by Olive Scott at hospital in July in the City of London." "I know I am dying." "Yes, Susan, I am reading verbatim, just listen." Joan's exasperated voice came up the stairs. "'I know I am dying and I have always feared the actual moment of death. But now it has really come, I realise I don't have to worry at all. I know I shall be with Christ and his multitude of angels in the next world and I am sure of this as I have been fortunate enough to meet one of those very angels before my death. I have met the Vicar of St Mary Abchurch. He has put my heart and soul to peace and rest. I now fear nothing and I thank God for that and for my long and happy life.'" Then there is a sort of scrawl. "I suppose she was trying to sign it but obviously hadn't the strength or indeed the energy. Well, after we had left the hospital, on the train home," Joan continued, "Aubrey held the prayer book very close to his chest, I noticed. He was very quiet, thinking deeply and I suspect he was inwardly praying; he looked at one point as though he was about to burst into tears. So I just didn't disturb him. One thing was odd though, before we left the hospital, the nurse asked to speak privately to Aubrey and she took him aside into a waiting room. I just stayed in the corridor. I don't know what was said and somehow I just didn't feel it appropriate to ask him at that moment."

Joan whispered something else, inaudible to Aubrey, and with that, she said goodnight to Susan and came upstairs. The vicar was already in bed and pretending to be asleep.

Chapter 8

August

August is an unremarkable month for secular businesses and enterprises. Holidays figure prominently on the nation's calendar and most parts of the broadcasting and print media scramble to produce new and exciting stories. The Established Church is likewise in the religious doldrums. The Sundays in the Book of Common Prayer grind on slowly through the weeks of the ecclesiastical season of Trinity. Any worshippers and ministers not on holiday were working at the sluggish pace which the hot weather dictated. And that year, the weather had indeed turned sultry, making the City squares look dusty, tired and no longer fresh. Retailers suffered the most, of course. as they found themselves caught in those few weeks between the current summer season and the upcoming autumn of the year. No one was in the mood to buy the cold weather clothes bought in bulk and overflowing in their bulging stockrooms. And the best items from the summer sales had long since been picked over. The general lack of energy affected everyone.

Rather unusually though and against the trend, this month of August was not difficult or sluggish at all for St Mary Abchurch. Indeed, it was probably the busiest period of the entire year so far. Every London tour guide had realised by now that Abchurch would always be open; they would no longer have to stand forlornly outside in the square. And more importantly, they and their groups would be guaranteed a friendly welcome. So they shepherded domestic and international tourists through the main door at an increasing pace. In fact, so many were the parties now wanting to see St Mary Abchurch that the guides had worked out an informal visiting schedule to give themselves free space inside and to avoid disturbing the growing number of services. The building also, as Joan had remarked before, was pleasantly cool in the relentless heat; a fact which the stream of overseas visitors also discovered that month.

In August, Aubrey, always trying to beautify his church and attract more communicants, decided to get some professional advice on the condition of the Abchurch bell. He had often mused on his earlier thought that St Paul's Cathedral would like to hear the voice of his Abchurch daughter, and idly flicking through the parish records one day he discovered that the last time the bell had actually been rung had been to herald in the new millennium at the end of 1999. Since then, it had been fixed immovable and silent to the tower wall. August was clearly a suitable month to get the professionals to investigate.

So he telephoned the representatives of Whitechapel Bell Foundry who duly appeared at the start of the month, climbed up the tower and made an inspection. The bell, it turned out, was actually ten years older than the church. It was stamped 1675 but now was coated in thick dust high up in the belfry.

Explaining everything later that evening to Joan, Aubrey had enthused about it.

"It's enormous, my dear. Well, not enormous compared with the bells of St Paul's Cathedral, of course," he corrected himself, "but still taking up a substantial part of the old tower."

"Now, I hope you haven't spoilt that new jacket you had for Christmas before last, Aubrey." Joan had vigorously brushed chalk off his sleeves. "Crawling up those narrow stairs into that dingy tower."

Aubrey was not to be deterred.

"My dear, the Whitechapel engineers tell me they can lower the bell down through the centre of the tower, cart it away and recast and retune it, or whatever the technical phrase is, and have it back with us before Christmas. What about that! We might have a bell baptism I think it's called here in St Mary Abchurch, perhaps during our first carol service here. What an occasion that would be! Perhaps, I might even ask the bishop to come here to bless the bell."

"I wouldn't give that lot up at the Cathedral the time of day, never mind blessing bells," said Joan.

"No, dear, don't say that," said Aubrey. "The bishop personally has always been kind to me and, after all, he did give us St Mary Abchurch to look after. I owe him a lot actually if I think about it."

Joan's face showed she was not convinced but she declined to argue. She wandered off quickly, turning around suddenly as she did so. "And how do you propose that we pay for all this work on the bell on top of the £25,000 and all the other expenses?" was her final comment.

The vicar of St Mary Abchurch was not to be deterred. In the middle of the month, workmen appeared with chains, trolleys and lifting equipment and they slowly dislodged the old bell and lowered it down the tower and eventually into their van which was strategically parked at the back of the church in Sherborne Lane. Word quickly went around Abchurch Square that matters of some historical importance were happening and the drinkers outside the Vintry pub swarmed around to the back of the building to watch. Joan followed them quickly and passed around a collection tin.

"Expensive work renovating old bells, ladies and gentlemen," she said. "This one dates to the period just after the Great Fire of London. Please take as many pictures as you like on your mobile phones. But do help us pay for the work."

And soon, Joan's efforts were well-rewarded. The collection tin noisily rattled full of coins and notes.

The removal of the old bell became very much an event for the extended Abchurch family. The man on the coffee cart took advantage of the situation to sell extra cups of latte and flat white; the Vintry increased its sales of larger to a thirsty public, and a journalist from the London Evening Standard happening upon the scene was able to snap many pictures for the later editions of his newspaper.

"Let's see your clerical collar, Vicar. Don't be shy," he said. "This is a positive church story. August is always such a dead month in the newspaper trade as I'm sure you can imagine."

Aubrey happily obliged and posed for various snaps, one by the side of the bell, one leaning on the wall of the church and then one pretending to drive off with the van.

Eventually, after much skilful twisting and pushing by the foundry men, the old bell was manoeuvred carefully from the back door of the tower and brought to rest on the back of the vehicle.

"Get up there, Vicar, and stand next to it," said one of the drinkers from the Vintry. "That would make a good photo. We will make you a film star yet."

Aubrey did as they suggested and everyone clapped, laughed and chatted amiably in the warm sunshine. The occasion was indeed a great success. That August was memorable indeed.

Aubrey had been right. Sunshine did add its own positive stamp on any situation. The foundry men from the Whitechapel factory told Aubrey and Joan that they were very welcome to join one of their Saturday tours of the bell works to see for themselves just what the process of recasting their bell involved. They promised to do so and the van then backed slowly down Sherborne Lane to prolonged cheering from the drinkers.

As the truck was vanishing towards King William Street, two men, looking official and carrying tape measures and clipboards, approached the church also from Sherborne Lane.

"Can I help you?" said the vicar amiably.

"Oh no. Ignore us, Padre," said one. "We are just doing a general survey of the buildings in this area. You have no objection if we have a look inside the church?"

"Of course not," said Aubrey. "The building is for everyone. The main door is around the other side, on the square."

"Yes we know, thank you," they replied.

The men proceeded to measure bits of the pavement, record figures and take pictures on their mobile phones of the side of the church. They then climbed the church steps on Abchurch Yard and went inside.

Joan, who had gone into the vestry when the bell engineers were leaving, suddenly appeared, somewhat agitated.

"Who are those men, Aubrey? What are they doing? They look as though they are measuring up the place for a fire sale. Did the diocese send them?"

"I'm not sure, my love," said Aubrey. "I didn't like to ask them. Doing some sort of survey of the buildings in this area, they said. I just assumed they were from the Corporation of London. Leave them alone. I'm sure they are all right. If the diocese had sent them, they would have told me first."

"Maybe," said Joan doubtfully.

One of the crowd of drinkers from the Vintry, who had overheard the two talking said, "I can tell you one is called Trevor. He does work for your lot, the Church of England. Our firm consulted him once when we wanted to buy some church property across the other side of the City behind Liverpool St Station. I'm sure he's one of your religious lot, isn't he?" he said helpfully.

"Really, oh is he?" said Joan. "Let me ask them what this is all about."

And she marched back quickly into the church only to find that she was too late. The two men had already quietly slipped away, sensing that their presence was starting to cause something of a stir.

In August too, Nancy, who had been introduced to Aubrey on that unfortunate day in April when the vicar had been interviewed by John and Adrian, came into St Mary's to talk about her wedding. She had not forgotten the occasion on

Cannon Street when the idea of a church wedding had first been mentioned by her friend Karen. And the idea had grown as she was now a regular communicant at Abchurch. But not coming from a Christian family, Nancy was unfamiliar with even the idea of having a church wedding and she had been rather worried about the whole process. Eventually, she had told herself that she wanted a church wedding because all her friends automatically had one. It was part of the process of being married and the Church of England was where everyone went. But she was still worried. The vicar always seemed so friendly but he might quickly know she was using the church as a convenience and he might object. Indeed, her cousin had left a village church in Dorset in a flood of tears only the previous year when the local rector had refused to let the building be used by 'just any waif and stray' as he had indelicately put it, for a convenient society wedding. The Vicar of St Mary Abchurch may just be one of those clergymen.

Aubrey, however, was very familiar with such situations and he quickly put Nancy at her ease. "You know, my dear, it really upsets me when I hear stories like that of your cousin. The Church of England is here as a state church to look after the spiritual needs of the whole English flock. I feel it is your right to be married in a church which is 'by Law Established' and it is my duty, if asked, to officiate. So think no more of it. I think it was the first Queen Elizabeth who refused to 'put windows into men's souls' as she expressed it, and I do the same. You feel a need to get Christ's blessing on your ceremony then who am I to refuse that or to question it? St Mary Abchurch is here for you."

So that was that. Nancy and her boyfriend came in regularly to see Aubrey and they listened patiently as he explained some of the tenets of the Christian faith. Both began to attend Matins on Sunday and were especially excited when the vicar published their marriage banns publicly, as was required of him, before the whole congregation on three consecutive Sundays.

The wedding was set for the last Saturday in September, to fit in with the cancellation of a reception event booked to be held in a hotel south of the river. Aubrey had smiled when Nancy had told him this.

"You are so honest, my dear," he had laughed. "Not many of my flock would have admitted that to me. I know how difficult it can be to get the right venue for a reception. I'm sure at St Mary Abchurch, we can accommodate your reception plans. Don't worry."

Nancy had blushed.

"Well, you are so honest yourself, Vicar. You inspire honesty in your congregation. And it's not going to be a massive occasion. We can easily get from the wedding here then across London Bridge to the reception. If necessary, we could even walk, assuming it's not raining, of course. And also, Vicar," she had continued, "looking through the Prayer Book which you leant me, I see that we will be getting married on St Michael and All Angels Day, on 29 September, Michaelmas. And I'm told that Michaelmas daisies are associated with that day so I will try to get as many bunches as possible to decorate the church. Wild flowers are a particular delight of mine."

Aubrey had agreed that the building would indeed look at its special best so decorated with Michaelmas mauve and yellow and he laughingly said he would do all he could to keep the day sunny.

That August was also not the usual unremarkable month for the Vicar of St Mary Abchurch because in the last week, a large official looking letter arrived from a lawyer in New York City. Aubrey had to sign for the buff-coloured envelope which he put on his desk in the vestry.

"Well," said Joan eventually, "if you don't open it, I will. Whoever is writing to us from America? We've never even been there either of us. We have never ever had even a postcard from the United States before today."

Aubrey sat staring at the envelope.

"You know, Joan," he said. "I suddenly realise what this may be about and it makes me tremble."

"Well, open it, Aubrey," said Joan. "If it's bad news, we need to deal with it calmly and quietly. It might even be good news. Perhaps you have won money on a horse."

Both laughed at such an impossible prospect and eventually Aubrey ripped open the letter. There were several pages inside of very expensive writing paper and the whole thing was beautifully typed. Stapled to the back of the enclosures was an American bank cheque with £25,000 clearly written across it and the instruction, *"Drawn on and payable at Lloyd's Bank, London, England, in Pounds Sterling."*

Aubrey sat and read the letter. Then he read it again. Then he read it a third time. Then he sat back and said nothing. Joan by now could no longer bear the suspense.

"Aubrey," she said. "This is a cheque for £25,000 payable to the Vicar of St Mary Abchurch. That's you. Whatever is happening? What's it for? What's been going on? What does the letter say? Please tell me."

"My dear, I'm in some kind of shock," said Aubrey. "Well, you remember that lovely lady, Olive Scott, I told you about, who was taken ill on King William Street early last month? It seems this letter is from her lawyer in New York. In fact, it seems to be a communication originally from her husband. Much of it is in legal talk as far as I can understand it but this bit is interesting. Let me share it with you." And the vicar read as follows. "Reverend Braithwaite, Vicar of St Mary Abchurch in the City of London. You don't know me, Pastor, but I am Roderick Scott from Amity, a small town in Arkansas, USA. You were very kind to my wife, Olive, in July around the time of her death. I'm sure you must remember the occasion. You stayed with her in the street before the ambulance arrived and apparently you talked and prayed with her. I'm not a religious man, you understand, Pastor, but whatever you said had a great impression on her and put her mind at rest at the last. She looked over a prayer book you gave her apparently and she dictated a letter to me written down by a nurse as she was dying in the hospital that same night. It's from that letter that I know all about your church and your Christian mission in London and I know that someone at City Hall as we call it in the USA has decided to close you down unless you find £25,000. My goodness, Reverend Braithwaite I have spent my life fighting such pen pushers who have no idea what life is really like down near the furnace. Your story made me so cross and very sympathetic. As per Olive's instructions, I am pleased to enclose a draft for £25,000. Mail it off to City Hall as soon as possible and a deep warm thank you from across the Pond.

And by the way, please do accept the money. It was Olive's very clear wish, Reverend Braithwaite, and I want your church to benefit. I might even manage to call in one day to say hello and thank you personally if I ever make it over there."

Aubrey and Joan sat quietly. They could hear Bob finishing his organ practice in the body of the church. Neither of them spoke until eventually Aubrey said, "That evening at Barts Hospital, the nurse told me to expect this. I didn't tell you because, well, I didn't really believe it was possible. I will send the cheque back, of course. It's just too much and I don't expect to receive extra payment as a vicar for just doing my duty. But I do appreciate the gesture, nevertheless."

"You will do nothing of the kind, Aubrey," said Joan. "It is money for the church, not for you personally, and it's a gesture which Olive Scott wanted to make. We owe it to her to accept it."

"The funny thing is that although I remember talking to her, of course, I just don't remember telling her about the £25,000," said Aubrey. "I must have just blurted it out as she lay on the street. It must have been uppermost in my mind. I will go by Lloyd's Bank in the morning to discuss it with them. £25,000! The dear, dear lady. How so very kind! She told me I was an angel but actually she is the angel. She's enabled St Mary Abchurch to stay open. Yes, you are right, I will keep the money but now I must write a long thank you letter to her husband in Arkansas and to the lawyer in New York City."

And he sat down at his desk indicating he wanted to be left alone to collect his thoughts.

Chapter 9

September

By September, with the annual holidays now finished, the offices around the church were quickly filling up with returning employees. And many joined the increasing number of services which Aubrey now provided. The church was indeed becoming so popular that a Communion service was held every lunchtime rather than just once or twice a week. And on Sunday, he had started to provide an early Parish Communion as well as the principal service of Morning Prayer and an end of day Evensong. In fact, the rapidly increasing number of services was becoming quite exhausting for both Aubrey and Joan. The latter had even decided to make good on her promise to arrange a Sunday school during the Matins Service for the many children who were now regularly being brought along to church by their parents.

One day in September, at breakfast, Joan remonstrated with her husband. "My dear, we must talk seriously about developments at Abchurch," she said. "We are both older people now and our retirement in a few years is inevitable. We know that even if we don't talk about it. But over the last two months, you have increased your workload by a sizeable amount, just at a time indeed when most of our friends are starting to reduce theirs. Look at today as an example. You have agreed to read The Litany after Evening Prayer. I know it's not a big imposition and you are merely fulfilling many requests. But such extra services need organising and add an additional burden on an already heavy week. I often do help out, it's true, but I am not a young woman anymore either. If you want to grow the congregation in this way, then you must ask the Diocese to provide someone to help you out; a young man or woman you might train and encourage at the same time. And think about it, Aubrey," she continued. "You don't run this place as a typical parish church in the Anglican communion is organised. We don't have a Parochial church council. We don't have church wardens and sidesmen and women to help out. I know you agreed to take over the church on that basis. Well, time has moved on. It is really time now that we did have support."

Aubrey readily agreed. Indeed, he had thinking something similar only the day before when he had realised that in his haste, he had entirely forgotten to organise the collection during the final hymn in the Matins Service. He had just so much on his mind to remember.

"Look, Joan," he said. "I have actually been giving a lot of thought as to how we restructure the church, to put it on a proper legal footing for the future. And there are a couple from the Matins Service whom I might approach to act as church wardens going forward. But really, this expansion of services, especially since the summer break, has taken even me by surprise. In a real sense, though, I feel we are both being swept along by events. I don't feel that it's me or indeed us who are growing the congregation. It is just happening. Something is stirring many of the people around about. We are only meeting demand. It's the work of the Lord. I firmly believe that."

"Well, that may be," agreed Joan. "However, that doesn't alter the facts. We are getting very busy, indeed, here at St Mary Abchurch. Added to which, don't forget in an average month you are now hosting a series of special services as well as the usual daily offices. In September, for example, we have the wedding service, remember? That will take a long time just to organise satisfactorily. And Nancy will expect the place to sparkle and look it's best, which, of course, it will do. But all this means extra work for us."

Aubrey sighed and laughed. "Of course, she will expect it and Abchurch will look its best as you know. Anyway, my mother used to say, 'It's better to wear out than rust out'. Oh we will be all right, you'll see. I will mention extra help to the diocese and ask Hattie and Robbie from the Sunday service if they would be willing to help us organise the place going forward."

"Well, perhaps yes," shrugged Joan. "But goodness only knows why you take on so much. Why did you have to suggest a special drink for the congregation after Evening Prayer on St Matthew's Day, for example? It's only a week or so before our big wedding, after all. And you know that even the merest hint of free alcohol will bring in that tribe from the Vintry next door. And someone will need to organise the event and clean up afterwards. In other words, us; Mr and Mrs Vicar!"

Aubrey looked downcast and said nothing. Later that day, robed in a cassock and surplice, he read slowly and carefully the words of the Litany asking the Lord for deliverance, to which the congregation dutifully replied, "Good Lord, deliver us," or other responses as noted in the prayer book. The measured words gave the minister and congregation much spiritual comfort and indeed such impromptu services were one of the reasons for the unlikely growth of the parish this late summertime. But Joan was right; it was all extra work at St Mary Abchurch. The facts had to be addressed.

The important occasion that September was, of course, Nancy's marriage. And the wedding itself turned out to be a magnificent event, one of those ecclesiastical occasions for which St Mary Abchurch seems to have been built. Helpfully, the weather continued warm which enabled the guests to look their summery best, and the church in turn to respond magnificently to their expectations. Freshly polished, she looked resplendent, smothered under a cascade of colourful flowers and plants which decorated the pulpit, pew ends, window ledges, and altar. Nancy was a firm and very vocal advocate of English wildflowers and as a consequence wild basil, brooklime, white campion and cornflowers, all flowering in late summer, adorned the building. Michaelmas daisies vivid with their yellow and purple predominated as the wedding was to be held on the feast day of St Michael and All Angels, the 29th of the month. The flowers spoke of happiness and their mood infected everyone as bride and groom were obviously so content and blissful to be together in each other's company. The bride in a specially made white Nottingham lace dress looked delicate and understated in a particularly English fashion. Everything looked constructed to show off the proceedings in a memorable light. Even the words of the marriage service itself seemed especially suited to that early autumn day in September.

"Look, Vicar," Nancy had said at the last rehearsal before the actual event. "I've talked to several members of my family and despite their advice and particularly in spite of all the negative things my father said, I think I want to maintain tradition and use the word 'obey' in the service on the day itself. As you know, The Book of Common Prayer states, 'Wilt thou obey him, and serve him, love, honour, and keep him in sickness and in health.' The words are so balanced and historical somehow, so I would like to say 'obey'. I've thought about this an awful lot. Please do let me."

Aubrey had laughed and tried to reassure her that no one said that nowadays but she was quite adamant. "I want to say 'obey' even if I'm not sure I mean 'obey' quite as Thomas Cranmer would have meant it all those years ago," she laughed.

The vicar had smiled, quite overwhelmed by her infectious humour.

"So be it, my dear. It's your day and 'obey' it shall be. It must be thirty years at least since I used that word in a wedding service."

The church was so full that Saturday that unusually the line of side box pews around the walls which faced inwards towards the main congregation had to be used and extra chairs were placed in the small upstairs gallery which itself was glistening with extra polish.

"All these people aren't coming to the reception," the groom had whispered to Joan before the service began. "We aren't that rich."

Joan had smiled while rearranging some last-minute deliveries of cornflower bouquets.

The hymns, of course, came from Hymns Ancient and Modern and Bob played the organ with a special vivacity and delicacy. Nancy had requested hymn number 766, 'Praise, my soul, the King of Heaven'. She had explained to Aubrey that this was important to her because it was used at her mother's wedding many years before but more importantly because quite by chance, she had stumbled across the grave of its author, Henry Lyte, in the churchyard of the Anglican Church in Nice on a recent cycling holiday in the south of France. She knew then that she had to have that hymn.

When everyone was ready and wedged into the very full pews, the vows were exchanged. The vicar spoke loudly and clearly. The ancient words of the Book of Common Prayer reverberated around the building as they had done for hundreds of years. Everyone in Sir Christopher Wren's church of course could see, hear and understand all the proceedings. The word 'obey' was used quite naturally and no one in the church looked uncomfortable with that. The day was sunny, and bright streams of yellow poured through the clear windows and lit up Aubrey's white surplice, which had been especially dry-cleaned for the occasion. Bob's choir sang a piece by Vaughan Williams as the bridal party signed the registers at an antique mahogany table especially set up for the occasion in the south east corner of the church.

Afterwards, to the strains of the Wedding March the guests poured out noisily and happily into Abchurch yard for the photographs, selfies and videos. And, of course, inevitably once outside, many of the guests threw confetti onto the couple. Nancy had rather worried about this beforehand because she knew from her office colleagues that many clergymen discouraged the practice. But Aubrey didn't mind.

"Don't worry, my dear," he had said. "Joan and I can easily sweep up when you've all gone."

Nancy had reminded him he was coming to the reception and it was important that he did so because he had promised to say a prayer before the meal.

"I will sort the confetti," Aubrey had laughed. "I think I can find someone to sweep up a bit of confetti. Please don't worry. It's your day. Just enjoy it."

Nancy had organised two old London red Routemaster double decker buses to carry the guests over London Bridge to the hotel for the reception.

"Cheaper to walk over the bridge, I know, and probably just as quick with the state of the traffic in the City. But these buses say London for me," she whispered to the vicar as they stood in the yard, as if to justify the expense to herself. "Just as the Prayer Book says England. That's what I always wanted on my wedding day. These are some of the things which I will always treasure and remember."

"Ah, well," laughed Aubrey. "Here's something else you can treasure as the years go by. Joan and I have arranged for a fine old Georgian print of St Mary Abchurch to be mounted and framed. It will be delivered to your workplace and be waiting when you both return from honeymoon."

Nancy brushed away the tears in her eyes. "Thank you so much. You must be the best, most considerate vicar in the whole of the Church of England," she said. And she leant over, squeezed his hand and kissed him.

Chapter 10

October

As all clergymen know, early October is always the time to celebrate Harvest festival. Days are shortening rapidly and this year although the sun still retained a noticeable warmth, there was a marked chill in the night air. Joan broached the matter of the harvest first.

"You realise, Aubrey, that we are duty-bound to organise a Harvest Festival Service During Matins," she said at the start of the month.

"Yes, of course," said Aubrey. "It will be the second Sunday of the month, I think. I will announce it this week."

"But how can we realistically have such a celebration here in the middle of the City of London? Hardly in the middle of corn fields, are we," she said dismissively. "St Mary Abchurch even in its wilder moments can't pretend that it's in the midst of a rural spot. I notice that the Vintry pub next door has a stuffed fox and a rabbit dressed as huntsmen with guns and field glasses in its side window. That's about as far as we extend to being in the countryside here."

"Yes, I did worry about that," said Aubrey. "Last week, I asked Bob and some of the choir for their advice. Our choir members have lived and worked in the City of London all their lives but they tell me they have always celebrated the harvest in neighbouring churches. And only last month, several in the Sunday congregation approached me to have a service. So the consensus seems to be that we should hold it, with the familiar hymns, of course, but perhaps ask people to bring toiletries and such like rather than the usual tins of beans and sacks of potatoes, which then we could distribute to the homeless charity hostels dotted on the edge of the Square Mile. Obviously, we would give them the takings from the collections on that Sunday as well."

So that was agreed and on the second Sunday of October, a large congregation came to Matins at St Mary Abchurch, weighed down with soaps, toothpaste, towels and talcum powder which were placed in piles throughout the building. The familiar hymns, beginning with 'We Plough the Fields and Scatter' were sung loudly and no one thought it incongruous to sing of fields of waving corn when Abchurch yard probably hadn't witnessed such a spectacle for many centuries.

As Bob explained, "It's all about giving to those in need, Vicar. And giving can come in many different forms."

After the service, a relay of excited parishioners was dispatched throughout the City carrying money and toiletries to the various homeless shelters. The day had really been worthwhile.

Unfortunately, the happy mood of Harvest soon vanished. By the middle of October, even Aubrey had started to notice that other churches in the City of London were tending to ignore both him and St Mary Abchurch. The parishes did operate separately as a rule but often various clergymen were in the habit of stopping by for a chat as they walked through the streets. And Aubrey indeed had occasionally visited parishes nearby to borrow matches or candles in an emergency. Suddenly, however, he was conscious that fellow clerics no longer popped in to say hello or even smiled at Aubrey when they passed him in the street. Indeed, once he thought he noticed that the minister from a church close by actually seemed to run into the traffic on King William Street just to avoid him. He tried to put the idea away from his mind and convince himself that he was imagining such a thing. Just the brain playing tricks, he told himself. The man was in a hurry. The clerics in the Church of England would not act in such an unchristian manner here in the Diocese of London. He was sure of that. After all, he had always been told that the City was very much a team of incumbents, each one looking out for their fellow priests. Indeed, as he understood it, this was one of the central tenets of FFA, Faith For All.

At the same time, independently, Joan also noticed a distinct cooling of her relationship with local church officials. She had previously often had occasion to chat amicably with them in the street on her trips to the bank or to Sainsbury's, or as she explored the various old churches in the City in the summer sunshine. But now, suddenly, she too felt that they often rushed by without speaking or as happened to her husband, they pretended not to see her.

In the middle of the month, on the eighteenth, by now rather agitated she brought the matter up with Aubrey as he was preparing the altar to celebrate holy communion on Saint Luke's Day.

"It seems to me, Aubrey," she said, "that our fellow churches are ignoring us all of a sudden. Maybe I'm getting paranoid in my old age, but I feel that we are being deliberately ostracised. Are we being shown that we don't really belong in the City of London? In fact," she continued, "the Methodist ministers from Wesley's Chapel on City Road are far more friendly now to me than people in the Anglican churches. I often have a coffee and chat on City Road nowadays."

Aubrey at first was dismissive of what Joan was saying but eventually, he had to admit to her that he had started to sense something of the same. He told her of his recent experience on King William Street.

"Even John over at St Mary le Bow pretended not to see me the other morning. I'm sure, he did. Perhaps, it's that the days are drawing in and not as warm as they were. Winter is coming on; people don't want to stand talking in the street," he said. "Although, thinking about it," he continued, "it is very strange that no one communicates about FFA now. I find that as odd as the fact that our fellow churches ignore us. We have not even had word from the diocesan office about progressing with Faith For All and the area dean has not brought me a new model of the dome of St Paul's as he promised. All I have is that broken thing on my desk. St Mary Abchurch was supposed to be a trial run for the project, or so I believe. Andrew was talking about working jointly with me."

"That's very interesting, Aubrey," said Joan. "Perhaps, the two are related. I do know that Faith For All is progressing because I popped into St Lawrence Jewry the other day and I overheard two of the officials talking about it. The vicar there is working day and night writing up his contribution apparently or so they said. And there is another conference being planned something offsite over a long weekend. No, the idea of Faith For All has not gone away. It's just that we here at St Mary Abchurch seem suddenly to have been excluded.

"Oh well, let's be positive," she laughed as she noticed Aubrey's obvious alarm. "I think they are rather envious of the success we are making of this place. Perhaps, they realise we have already achieved much of FFA on our own. We don't need offsite conferences and long weekends to push forward the gospel. Such occasions are often the scene of much back-biting, or so I believe. I remember when my father used to organise his annual arts festival, several deans from other cathedrals made acerbic comments about him and the festival over their free glasses of wine when they attended our receptions. As a young girl, I often heard them. It always seemed odd and very unkind to my way of thinking to accept someone's hospitality then to say nasty things about them at the same time."

"Now please, no thoughts like that, Joan. Christianity is not a competition," exclaimed Aubrey. "We are all welcome at Christ's banquet. The Lord's House has many mansions. We aren't the only growing church around in spite of what you say. And, after all, you never know what handicaps my fellow ministers have to work under. We were not put here to sit in judgement. No one envies any of us working in the ministry, of that I'm sure. Let's just continue on our own with our Christian mission. And as for offsite meetings, after all as you know, I'm not someone who performs well in such marketing type programmes and conferences anyway."

Having said this, he hurried past his wife to set up the altar for the lunchtime holy communion.

Later on, during the service, Joan was listening to him reading the words of the collect.

'Almighty God, who calledst Luke the Physician, whose praise is in the Gospel, to be an Evangelist, and Physician of the soul.'

She heard no further. She just couldn't concentrate on the service as the discussion with Aubrey rolled round and round in her head. She decided to go out into the sunshine and not take communion that day at all.

Once in the churchyard, she bought a cappuccino from the coffee cart and sat drinking it on one of the seats near the main door of the church, enjoying the warm autumn sunshine on her face. At that moment, from Selborne Lane she saw a workman appear whom she thought she recognised as one of those engineers who were measuring in the church a couple of months before. She decided to find out exactly what was going on, so she rushed up to him, spilling her coffee as she did so and said, "Excuse me, can I have a word with you? I believe you were doing some measurements in our church here a few weeks ago. What exactly was that all about?"

The man stopped and looked at her startled. He blushed and stammered.

"I'm not sure how much you know. I really don't know what I should say. It's not up to me to say anything. I think you should ask the area dean about all this. We are acting on his instructions. I can say though that we are doing an architectural audit of some of the church property in this part of the City of London. I believe the Church of England is looking to put some sort of new plan in place for propagating the gospel in the diocese of London, and all I know is that I'm working on the building side of the scheme. I think they call it FFA. I'm not sure what that means. Anyway, I'm sorry, I'm late. I really must run."

The engineer smiled and moved away quickly.

Later that afternoon, after the service was finished and the prayer books tidied away, Joan told Aubrey of her discussions with the engineer and said that it would be a good thing if both of them perhaps made an appointment with the area dean to find out exactly what this was all about. It might even have something to do with the fact that they were being ostracised by the rest of the clergy around about. It was time to clear the air.

"Oh, I really don't think so," said Aubrey quite alarmed. "You always see conspiracies everywhere. But I agree it is true that my conversation with the area dean is very much in abeyance and it is odd that he hasn't returned here. On reflection, following our unfortunate altercation in the summer it is probably time that we got back together to discuss how FFA should progress. At least I would be appearing to show interest. If I'm honest, I don't like being left out in the cold and forgotten. I will arrange a meeting with the area dean over the next couple of weeks. And you really don't need to be there, Joan." He shuddered. "I will handle this myself. Perhaps, I will mention that St Paul's model at the same time."

Later that afternoon, he decided to walk down Cannon Street to make an appointment. He needed the exercise and he felt it was often more beneficial for both parties if there was actually a meeting rather than a brief telephone conversation.

He ambled down Cannon Street, chatted to two parishioners from his Matins Service who were leaving Marks and Spencer's and was soon at St Paul's Cathedral and pressing the bell at the diocesan offices. Rather surprisingly, the area dean himself answered. Shocked at seeing Aubrey, he visibly scowled.

"Oh you're here from St Mary Abchurch, are you, Mr Braithwaite, Reverend Braithwaite I mean?"

"Yes," said Aubrey. "I thought as we hadn't really concluded our chat over FFA, I should get back together with you to see how we take the plan forward. I believe that other churches are putting contributions into the overall FFA plan and I remember you said that Abchurch ideally should be one of the first in the scheme."

The area dean, unprepared, looked bewildered and flustered.

"There is so much going on at the moment," he stuttered, leaving Aubrey standing on the doorstep. "This FFA plan is taking up so much of my time. I can't really arrange a one-to-one meeting with you in the near future. It would make more sense for us to plan to get together for a larger discussion perhaps with John and Adrian, say in a month's time at the end of November. That sounds a good time and we will all have our thoughts together then about the way forward both for you personally and for your church. I think that's the best way to proceed, Reverend Braithwaite; a longer more relaxed chat over a cup of tea."

"About me personally? What do you mean, Andrew? You've got me a bit worried," said Aubrey rather dismayed and no little shocked.

"Look, I can't say anymore now. I will get my secretary to fix a date with you for the end of next month. Sorry, I must go. Very busy this afternoon." The area dean closed the door and left Aubrey standing on the office steps.

Aubrey walked slowly back up Cannon Street, deep in thought. "This was a funny turn of events. A discussion about the way forward for St Mary Abchurch presumably meant FFA but then a discussion about himself. Was he under some sort of censure? Had someone complained about him? He thought about what the area dean had said over and over again.

He had not expected to see the area dean in person today and he certainly had not expected to hear that he was to be invited in for a detailed chat, especially one which might include elements of his own position. He sensed trouble. It took him a long time to walk back up Cannon Street towards the church. On this occasion, he went into several of the shops to buy sweets or to look at the various items on sale just as a way of passing the time so he could think.

Back at St Mary Abchurch, Joan was locking the main door when Aubrey turned into Abchurch Square. She could see he was deep in thought and she was suddenly worried.

"I was going to come along Cannon Street to look for you. Did you arrange the appointment, Aubrey?" she asked.

"Yes, my dear, I did. His secretary will ring me but it will be arranged for some time at the end of November just before Advent Sunday," he sighed.

"Why the morose expression then?" she continued, grabbing hold of his arm.

Aubrey gave a brief outline of his discussion with the area dean. "Why do they want to talk about my role? And why was I left standing in the doorway of the diocesan offices?" He looked sadly at Joan. "I can't help thinking that we will be pushed out of Abchurch. I don't believe they have someone to take over from us. We are blocking some development. No, it must be they have other plans for the place. We had assumed that this move to St Mary Abchurch would be our last appointment but perhaps that's not to be. Perhaps we will have to move somewhere else, to another parish for my final three or four years in the ministry."

Joan silently finished locking up. "Come on, cheer up. Let's have a glass of cream sherry at the Vintry," she said. "There, at least, we are among friends."

Later, sitting together in a warm corner of the bar, and fortified by two glasses of sherry, she continued, "I suspect they may want to encourage us to retire early, not let us move to another parish. That is what I think, Aubrey. Goodness only knows what they have written in your personnel file. We must be blocking something. Well, if I'm right, so be it. We have our own house and much of my parent's money in the bank. But I do really believe they are annoyed because of our success here. That's what all this is about. You just work as a clergyman as you were brought up to do but that no longer fits in with their modern plans. It would have been so much easier for them if we had failed in our mission. They put us up to fail and then they could tell the Archbishop they had really tried to make St Mary Abchurch successful as a modern church. Unfortunately, it had just not turned out as they hoped. Something else must now be done with the site."

"Here you go again, Joan! You spend too much time thinking things over," said Aubrey. "Sometimes, I despair that you were ever raised in a deanery at all."

And with that, Mr and Mrs Vicar joined the lively evening crowd at the other side of the Vintry pub, although neither was able completely to forget the words of Andrew Grist.

Chapter 11

November

In November, the weather suddenly turned cold and damp. The dry warm sunshine of autumn was quickly forgotten as the nights lengthened, encroaching relentlessly on the short daylight moments. Aubrey, of course, kept the lights burning and the heat turned on in the church to ensure that the place continued to be a welcoming beacon of Christian pilgrimage and rest to all who needed it.

Early in the month, Sunday Matins was extended to include a Service of Remembrance for those fallen in war which was exceptionally well-attended and included as guests representatives of the City Police as well as the armed forces with their flags and musical instruments. And it was especially pleasing to the vicar that the lady who had been married in St Mary Abchurch in 1945 also turned up with a few of her Royal Navy friends, all now very old indeed. When she arrived, she sought out the vicar and asked if they could sing the sailors' hymn, "Eternal Father, Strong to Save", and Aubrey, of course, was only too pleased to add it at the end of the service as a special memento for the dear lady and all peoples associated with the sea.

At the last moment, with only minutes to go before the processional hymn, representatives of a French television channel also appeared and asked if they might film bits of the service for a documentary they were making on the current state of Christianity in the United Kingdom. Aubrey was somewhat flustered at the request, coming as it did as he was trying to welcome all his other guests.

"It's rather last minute," he blustered. "But if you don't disturb the proceedings too much, I suppose it will be all right."

"Oh with modern digital equipment, Padre, you won't even know we are around and we might even do a bit of a profile on you." They reassured him as they quickly and discretely positioned their cameras upstairs and near the main altar. "Some of our contacts told us that Abchurch was rather different from the usual church so we just had to come along. The word is, Padre, that you actually have a large congregation. We couldn't find too many other churches in London like this."

Throughout the rest of the month, the vicar continued with his clerical duties as was required of him but he couldn't help but ponder and worry about the meeting in the Diocesan offices scheduled for the last week of November. He expected it would be a miserable, difficult occasion when he would be lectured to and treated patronisingly. He had come to expect nothing less. And as he had got older, he had sensed that even the little fight he had within himself was draining away. He was still glad he was a minister and enjoyed helping his parishioners but if he were honest with himself, he was starting to feel that he was no longer up to the political and religious battles enjoyed by younger men and women.

Perhaps he should retire, he told himself that November, he was only three or four years from retirement anyway, but then again, he assured himself, that he often pondered this idea at the dark end of the year and by the spring, he had usually bounced enthusiastically back into his working life. This year though did feel slightly different.

One day, thoughtfully over breakfast, he told Joan that the ministry was meant for young men and women. People who could stand up straight and do battle. Joan had nearly choked on her toast. She had no qualms about fights. Looking at her across the table, Aubrey secretly felt that she seemed to enjoy strife – no, he didn't mean that really. But it was true that she considered all political angles to a problem in a way that he could never do, never wanted to do. Whatever her age and whatever time of year, she was obviously still determined to keep fighting and, indeed, it seemed that such skirmishes with the ecclesiastical authorities gave her a purpose in life.

"Look, Aubrey, you are always like this as the nights draw in," she said. "We have created what some are saying is the best-attended, most vibrant church in the City of London. And we have done this in less than a year. The two of us with the organist and one or two volunteer helpers have become something of a small team." And she continued, "You told me Abchurch was welcoming us in January. Do you remember? And I admit I dismissed the notion as just you being sentimental. Well, perhaps you were right, and I was wrong. Perhaps, we were destined to make a success of this place. In my own defence, I might add that I did say to my father and grandfather all those years ago, that you would be a senior official in the Church. With a bit more gumption," she added as an afterthought. "Well, we now even have that French television channel, the ones who came along to the Remembrance service, asking to do a profile on us here at St Mary Abchurch. That will be quite something when the bishop finds out about it, won't it? Even my father was never on television."

Aubrey had to agree that it was very flattering and it was nice to see how many people from all walks of life came into Abchurch on a regular basis. He smiled to himself.

"It was really funny when that tourist wrote in the visitors book that our church was so busy that it had become the 'Piccadilly Circus' of the Anglican Communion."

"Look here," said Joan. "I know you are worried about your meeting at the end of the month. I can sense you lie awake thinking about it. That is the basis of your dark mood, isn't it?" She didn't expect an answer and she continued, "Well, I'm not going to suggest that I come along with you on this occasion."

As Aubrey looked startled she continued, "Frankly, my advice is that you go to the diocesan offices, listen to what they say and afterwards, we will work out the future together."

She squeezed his hand and smiled.

"After all, if they want to get rid of you, they will have to give you a decent pension and that with my family money means we are not going to be poor in old age, are we? My grandfather used to say, 'When you have money in the bank, you don't need to call anyone 'sir'."

Aubrey laughed and felt a tear in his eye.

"It would be nice in a few years to have a small place in a country area away from London. And who knows when we are there, I may even be able to occasionally help the local vicar, one of those ministers we read about who are struggling to run four or five parishes. I won't need to be paid after all. But first things first. We aren't quite ready for retirement yet. We haven't even been here for a year. And I'm quite determined to hand over a vibrant St Mary Abchurch to the next incumbent."

He suddenly felt better and rushed off to open up the church.

The meeting at the offices near the cathedral had been fixed for the last week of the month, between 'Stir up' and Advent Sundays, the last and first Sundays of the Church's year. The 25th Sunday in Trinity had always been an occasion relished by Joan. She insisted on calling it 'Stir Up Sunday' as had her parents before her, after the words of the Collect according to the Book of Common Prayer and she knew that she was following centuries of Protestant tradition by stirring her Christmas puddings on that date.

"Stir up, we beseech thee, O Lord, the wills of thy faithful people," she mouthed silently as she made her puddings on that dark day in November.

On this Sunday, though, she was preparing her puddings with little real enthusiasm. She could sense that in spite of her encouragement, Aubrey had a lot to think about as he had been so quiet after closing the church following matins.

"You know, Aubrey," she started hesitatingly as she stirred, "I was thinking to help you put a few ideas on a piece of paper like last time, before you go to meet the area dean. But now I think about it as I stir this pudding I don't see the need. What have you got to prove after all? The only real thing to think about is at what point in the meeting do you present the cheque to him, the £25,000."

"Look here," said Aubrey crossly as he took a turn stirring the pudding, "I will give them the cheque right at the beginning. In fact, the family purse is long overdue and I should have sent if off before this. They have a right to the money after all. You do exasperate me sometimes, Joan. I will just give them the cheque and that's an end to it."

"Oh no, Aubrey, you don't do that! After how you have been treated. No, how we both have been treated. You have to play this right. Present it at the right moment to maximum effect. Mind you, I wouldn't really have wanted to be vindictive," she hesitated thoughtfully, "had I not overheard Sheila from St Botolph telling someone last Wednesday that the Vicar of St Mary Abchurch would have got further in the Church of England if it wasn't for the fact that his wife had had extramarital affairs with various church wardens. I was so upset when I heard this that I didn't know what to do, Aubrey. They hadn't spotted me. I started to tremble, and rushed into the street. It made me so cross and embarrassed. But then I began to think, I wonder if Aubrey himself assumes that."

"Assumes what?" asked Aubrey.

"That I have had affairs in our married life and that such relationships have held you down at the bottom of the ecclesiastical ladder," she said.

This was the first time the matter of the church warden in the previous parish had actually been broached between them. The room fell silent. Aubrey could hear the kitchen clock beating time on the wall. Looking up, he could see that Joan was upset and a tear was dropping into the pudding as she stirred it. He suddenly felt tender towards her and smiled reassuringly.

"My dear," he said, "any fault is all mine. I don't feel that I am at the bottom of any ladder. That's the way your father used to speak and your grandfather, if I can be truthful. And as for us, honestly we don't talk enough together, you and I. I spend more time with my parishioners than I do with you. I'm so much at fault. I hear silly things said now and then, but I never really listen even when I hear them. Such nastiness goes straight through my head. Being a clergyman at least teaches you that lesson, or should do. I think it's in the Epistle of James that we are warned that no man can tame the tongue which is unruly and full of deadly poison. I always feel that thought goes straight to the centre of much of modern life. No, Joan, you are the main thing in my ministry; you, dear. I decided that years ago and it's still true." And he leaned across and kissed her.

Joan continued slowly stirring the Christmas pudding.

"Aubrey, you are not at the bottom of anything. I realise that now. Old age has perhaps brought me some maturity," she reflected. "Yes, I suppose there was a time when I wanted you to be important in the Church of England but actually, does all that really matter? As you would say, 'Is that really what Christ wants?' I see the way you react with all who come to St Mary Abchurch and the way they like you and keep coming back to the place. And my goodness, as I said the other month the size of the congregations here could mean you might justifiably request the services of a curate to help you out. You are not a young man now, you know. You have built a seriously large church for all age groups and I think that is very much against the trend elsewhere."

She continued, "I walk around the City of London more than you do and I can tell you the churches here are pretty much empty, except for tourists, with one or two exceptions perhaps. So actually, I'm proud of you, Aubrey. And I really think you are right. We are doing the Lord's work here."

She smiled and put the last of the puddings in a saucepan on the cooker, ready to be steamed.

"Oh, but Aubrey," she added as an afterthought. "I must say this. In those meetings, always attack, don't defend. When you see that Philip or Andrew or whatever his name is, the area dean, emphasise to him that you do warrant a curate to help out here. Don't just diffidently suggest the idea. Forcefully tell him."

The following Wednesday afternoon found Aubrey sitting in the diocesan reception room. This time taking Joan's advice, he had decided against bringing a piece of paper. He would only lose it in his haste and no doubt be the butt of jokes because of it after the meeting. But on Joan's firm instruction he was wearing his best dark business suit and a new bright clerical collar. Indeed, he looked very smart. Joan had reminded him to take the cheque for £25,000 which was now pressed inside his suit pocket.

As he was sitting there, a side door opened and suddenly the bishop appeared. Seeing Aubrey, he became flustered, tried to smile, half murmured a greeting and then rushed out from the main door in obvious embarrassment.

A secretary came in, asked if he wanted a coffee, which he declined, and took him through to one of the larger conference rooms. There at one end of a large magisterial mahogany table sat John and Adrian on either side of a very sombre-looking Andrew Grist, the Area Dean.

John motioned a welcome to Aubrey.

"Ah now then, Reverend Braithwaite, very good to see you. Sorry it's been so long since we last met. Please sit down."

And he indicated a hardback chair a few feet away on its own by the fireplace.

Aubrey smiled and was about to say that they didn't need to be formal but this time he stopped himself.

"Good to see you all too," he said in his most relaxed manner.

"Reverend Braithwaite, we all hope this won't be a difficult conversation but there are one or two things we want to achieve—" John continued.

"My goodness, why should it be difficult?" interrupted Aubrey. "We are all disciples of Christ at the end of the day."

"Eh, yes. Well, we want to have a broader discussion with you. We want to talk to you about the developing church," said John. "You see, Reverend Braithwaite, the Church of England like all Christian religious denominations is changing rapidly. Added to which, as you know, we are now in a highly digital age and the message of Christ often has to get out by email, text or video. The old notion of churches as the focal point of a parish and people attending Matins and Evensong each Sunday has vanished. That's all there is to say. We have to adjust to this new reality. That was one of the messages of FFA, Faith For All, earlier in the year, but sadly you couldn't attend," he added coldly as an indifferent afterthought.

The area dean shot him a cautionary glance. "What I meant," said John, rapidly. "Is that we have spent a long time thinking through a new paradigm on how to connect with people in this digital age and to be blunt, your antiquated notion of the vicar in his parish church just does not relate anymore to the general public. So many of the churches in the City of London are just expensive museum pieces and they are now a hindrance, not a help in spreading the gospel of Jesus Christ."

He paused for breath as one with authority and looked for support to his two colleagues. But to no avail. Andrew and Adrian were staring at their shoes, both obviously feeling somewhat hot and embarrassed. Aubrey for his part said nothing. He just stared and continued to listen.

"Look here," blurted John, sensing the occasion was not developing as he and the others had planned earlier that morning. "What I mean to say is that you have tried to put a congregation into St Mary Abchurch, even your strongest critics would acknowledge that, and, indeed, I have heard that a few people sometimes do go there as a quiet place to use their mobile phones."

As he said this, he realised that his attempt at humour had fallen very flat indeed.

"Look, perhaps we weren't being very fair to give you that old place – it was locked up, wasn't it, I seem to remember – and then expect you to create a congregation for it. Not fair at all, especially as you are about to retire in the next few weeks."

He sat back.

"Am I about to retire?" questioned Aubrey, sitting now on the edge of his seat. "I'm still three and a half years off 70. Surely that is the retirement age in the Church of England, isn't it?"

John shifted uncomfortably on his chair and looked down at his notes.

"I think what John means," the area dean came to the rescue, "is that inevitably, after a long career, you must be approaching retirement and that your retirement, when it does come as it obviously must for us all, should be seen against a backdrop of rapid social change. Look, Reverend Braithwaite, let us be frank. This is a new age, and we need new men."

"And women," interjected Adrian.

"Oh yes, indeed." The area dean wiped his brow. "Clerical men and women who are naturally and automatically versed in all the technologies of the age and are happy to use them. Reverend Braithwaite, without being too personal, may I ask if you have a smart phone or even a basic mobile phone?"

Aubrey admitted that he did not and had never used one.

"The key pads are just too small for my chubby fingers." He smiled.

"Well, any congregation nowadays will have devices like that, and computers and iPads and the like. And furthermore," continued the area dean now feeling more confident, "as you know, we are experimenting with newer forms of church service, and with more up-to-date versions of the Bible. In fact, I say experimenting but as we all know such experiments have been in progress for many years. It is all very well to use the Book of Common Prayer and the King James Bible and they do have their place at great civic events like coronations and the like, of course. But let's be honest, no one today is going to come to church to listen to words from the Book of Common Prayer. Young people in the twenty-first century will just think it's a pompous irrelevance, couched in language they don't understand and haven't the time or inclination to learn. You must appreciate what I'm saying, surely."

"I'm afraid I don't understand at all," said Aubrey, feeling his neck starting to turn red. "I've always used the Prayer Book, it's true. Indeed, when I agreed to take that living, John here told me that I could use any form of service approved by the Church and—"

"Yes, yes, no one is saying you can't legally use the old forms," the area dean interrupted. "But my point is you shouldn't want to. I came to see you in the summer. Do you remember? And you were using the old prayer book. I was quite shocked."

"As is my right according to Canon Law," interjected Aubrey.

"Yes, yes quite. Please listen to what I'm saying. It's not a matter of law. It's beyond law."

The area dean, clearly cross, was almost spitting his words now.

"The point is you will never have a regular modern congregation at St Mary Abchurch if that's what you use. The Book of Common Prayer just will not do. The sixteenth century is hardly relevant to the twenty-first." The area dean wiped his brow.

"But I have built up an enormous congregation spread over a variety of weekday and weekend services," said Aubrey defensively. "And I only ever use the Prayer Book. I have regular communicants from virtually all sides of London and, in fact, two ladies come up to matins each Sunday from as far away as Dover, can you believe. Travelling by train all that way for the Book of Common Prayer? I have a large class in training for Confirmation next year and an active Sunday School, which my wife now runs. How many Sunday schools do you have in the City of London? I was actually today going to suggest to you that I might have a curate to help me out because of the pressure of work at St Mary Abchurch. As you say, I am not a young man anymore. And do you know there is a French television channel which is so impressed at what we are doing and with the size and diversity of our congregations that they may probably make a film on Abchurch and the way we promote our Christian message?"

Aubrey leaned back in his chair.

The area dean looked at John quite startled, not knowing what to find more alarming; the idea of an additional curate or the attentions of a French television channel. He opted for the latter.

"French television. We didn't know this," he said. "You should always tell the press office when something like this happens."

"Yes, my mistake," admitted Aubrey. "It all happened so quickly. I had meant to do so but in the excitement it quite slipped my mind. They filmed our Remembrance Service earlier this month and things just developed from there."

Andrew Grist looked at John who was making a note on his iPad. And feeling that he also was losing control of the meeting said, "Perhaps you might like to come back into the discussion here, John."

"Well," said John curtly, looking through his papers and changing tack. "Reverend Braithwaite, the bottom line is not really about prayer books. I'm afraid as the area dean will agree, it comes down to money. Sorry to seem crude and calculating but as you must know in many aspects of life it usually does. Buildings such as St Mary Abchurch do not pay for themselves. Yes, you heat and light the place and no doubt effect a few running repairs to the fabric but what about the

Common Fund? We need your church to pay towards the central costs of the diocese, the clerical and administrative salaries and the like, and even I might point out your own salary and future pension. And looking at the notes I made after our meeting in April, we did agree that the rate for St Mary Abchurch would be £25,000 for this year and for each year after that with an annual increase for inflation, of course. To be candid, Reverend Braithwaite, today we are asking you where is the Common Fund, Family Purse payment for your church. How do you expect the diocese to pay for your salary if we never receive any parish contribution to central funds? How do you expect St Mary Abchurch to stay open without that?"

He looked around at the area dean and Adrian, and all three smirked involuntarily.

Aubrey for his part in the stress of the moment had quite forgotten the cheque. He hastily reached inside his jacket and took out the draft for £25,000.

"Oh sorry," he said. "I had meant to give this to you when I arrived. I quite forgot." And he stepped forward and handed the cheque over to John. "That covers us until the end of next month, December, I think."

And he sat back in his chair.

John looked down at the draft with £25,000 printed clearly on it. He said nothing, not even a word of thanks. Adrian and Andrew were yet again looking straight at their shoes. The bracket clock on the Georgian sideboard ticked away the half seconds. No one spoke. John continued to look at the cheque, then he turned it over and examined the back.

Eventually, Aubrey broke the silence and laughed nervously.

"It's quite genuine. Lloyd's Bank will honour it. I assure you. And to speak to your earlier point, we at St Mary Abchurch know, of course, that we have to pay our way."

"Well, I'm not sure this really changes much," blurted out John eventually, sensing his face was turning very red. "We are in lengthy discussions with a property group about the premises, the church and the yard area. It's all part of a major redevelopment which might provide serious funds for the diocese."

"What!" exclaimed Aubrey. "Whatever are you saying, Reverend John? Area Dean, are you aware of this? What sort of discussions? Ah, was that those men walking around with tapes and rods measuring up the place a few weeks ago? My wife thought it was all rather odd at the time. I think we need to talk more widely on this subject. Property Group! Does the bishop know about your property group? Does the Archbishop of Canterbury know? Do the senior clergy in the diocese know? Does the BBC know perhaps is a better question. Our French television channel will be very interested in this. It's a nationally protected architectural jewel. Is St Mary Abchurch to be the first of many such sales?"

Aubrey had never been so agitated and consequently verbose in his entire working life. He was not to be halted now he was in full flow. Seeing Reverend John was about to speak again, he went on.

"St Mary Abchurch is one of Sir Christopher Wren's jewels. I've heard many tour guides get so excited about the place. They point out the ceiling, the reredos, the symmetry of the very building. The fact that Wren had been practising there before taking on the larger project of the dome of St

Paul's Cathedral. Talking to a property group! I just can't believe it! Will it become the Abchurch tower block? Some might argue the City of London has too many of those already. Will you even be selling St Paul's Cathedral next! Do you have no sense of the history of this great City and country?"

Sitting there, Aubrey suddenly understood the relevance of what his wife had been saying over many years. He now knew that she had been right all along. Not only did life come down to money, that much was quite apparent, but in addition, you just couldn't trust the church authorities. He and Joan had to fight for themselves and alongside, fight for Wren's church as well.

"Please don't upset yourself, Reverend Braithwaite," said John.

"Upset myself! I have laboured all my life since leaving school for the Church of England with very little encouragement from the senior officials in the ministry. Indeed, senior clergymen often look down on me because I didn't go to university and so can't wear an academic hood over my surplice. But, nonetheless, I have toiled in all weathers and in many church buildings, working with all types of people, mostly lovely Christian men and women, it's true, but sometimes with a tiny few very unpleasant people indeed. I was physically attacked one dark night in a previous parish church and had to spend several days in hospital. I've been spat at, laughed at and ridiculed for my faith. I frequently spend my own money to help unfortunate rough sleepers. In the tube, someone made fun of me once over his sandwich lunch. I constantly sit through interminable parish meetings which I have to try and make sense of, late at night when everyone has gone home. I often can't afford to take holidays but I know I'm doing the Lord's work and I don't complain. And I might add, my wife, unpaid as she is, has helped me in all this endeavour. And now after so many years and inevitably I agree somewhere near the end of my career, I find that no one in authority cares about or even knows what I have achieved or worries about the building I work in, which by the way I have to say I don't find a hindrance to spreading the message of Christ – quite the opposite. And if I do have critics as you suggest I have, then I'm sure they will agree with the things I'm saying."

"Furthermore," he continued, "although I wasn't going to mention this today, I might as well point out that no one from the diocese ever comes to one of my services – not even earlier this month when we celebrated Remembrance Sunday with the Royal British Legion and the Commonwealth War Graves Commission. They could turn up with their flags and wreaths but not senior clerics. The place was packed solid. And you were all invited. I distinctly remember that. You each got personal letters from me and you weren't even courteous enough to reply. Well, that's not quite true," he said as an afterthought, "one vicar here in the City did berate me for addressing him incorrectly on the envelope. And actually, now I think about it, you could have met the French television people at that service. They could find the time to come along from as far away as Paris to film the event, not just a quick walk down Cannon St. And today, I hear that you are going to knock down our gem of a church. And just as we are about to baptise the refurbished old bell. Oh this is all too much!"

"Look, Aubrey," said the area dean, suddenly trying to calm down the situation. "No one will knock down the church. You have my word on that." He looked sternly at John. "I think what Reverend John meant was that there has to be a financial element even to the Christian faith. But he has probably spoken rather too hastily. The Church is obviously not just about money, of course. And I have to tell you that I did know about the talks he mentioned and those discussions with the property group are over a whole range of issues we can't go in to today. But I can assure you that nothing has been signed off with them yet as far as St Mary Abchurch is concerned. That building is too important, and indeed nationally protected as you say, to even think of any serious alterations. You do have my word on that."

He looked sternly at Adrian and John.

"But time moves on and today we really wanted to make you an offer of a lump sum and an enhanced pension should you wish to leave and take early retirement say before the end of the year. I know it's quick and sounds a bit rushed but we have so many problems swirling around the diocese that it would actually be a big help if you were to assist us here. We would obviously show our appreciation for any accommodation you could make. But let me emphasise again, it's really up to you. Just give us a minute, please."

And he joined John and Adrian in a heated huddle at the end of the room. Whispers flowed and documents and letters were passed back and forth with many hasty amendments made. After a few minutes, the area dean came back.

"I have to be honest and candid, I did have some figures in mind today to offer you a pension topped up by a small clerical bonus but in the light of our discussions, perhaps I will give further thought to both and after redrafting my letter, send it on to you through the post," he said.

He stood up, clearly relieved the interview was at an end. He offered his outstretched hand to Aubrey.

"Thank you for your work in the Church, Reverend Aubrey. You have done a great service to the Church of England and on behalf of the bishop, I want to acknowledge that with some gratitude. As I say, we will be in touch further at a later date. And thank you for the cheque. With the state of current diocesan funds, your Family Purse contribution is very welcome indeed."

Aubrey shook his hand and walked out into the cold autumn air. It was now fully dark and crowds were pushing down the thoroughfares near the cathedral in their eagerness to take buses and trains home to the suburbs. *So after all these years, he thought I am going to be pensioned off.* He stepped to one side to avoid a plump man with his arm outstretched, hailing a taxi. This was it. He knew that really in spite of what the area dean had said, he had no real choice. He couldn't stay in post and defy the bishop. The decision, as quick as it was, had been made probably months ago; he was in the way of some expensive project and had to be removed. Well, so be it. He was too proud to beg for a different outcome. And moving to yet another parish somewhere for three years wasn't really an attractive proposition anymore. St Mary Abchurch was intended to be their final move. Joan and he had agreed on that a year ago after all.

He thought about the meeting as he walked back up Cannon Street. He realised, of course, that retirement is always a shock when it finally comes no matter how much preparation one has made. He remembered that he had told this to many parishioners over the years when he had counselled some who had felt they were being discarded, of no further use to society. Now it was the turn of Joan and Aubrey. That was all there was to say.

When he got back to St Mary Abchurch, the lights were still burning brightly. He told Joan the details of the meeting, leaving out the highlights of his own outburst.

"You were right, my love," he said dejectedly. "I should have listened to you a bit more over the years. The realities of life have finally caught up with me. I'm just an old fool of use to no one."

Joan squeezed his hand and smiled.

"Oh my love, the future's not dark, Aubrey. Quite the opposite. It will be a real wrench to leave St Mary Abchurch, I have to admit. But we have made some lasting friends here and after all, remember we have crammed such a lot into our few months. In fact, in many ways I sometimes have to pinch myself to realise that it is such a short time since I trod on the dead mouse that day."

They both smiled.

"And if as it seems we do have to go," she continued, "we will be leaving on an ecclesiastical high, Aubrey. I think this has been our best and most spiritually rewarding parish. And I mean that. And you mark my words, they are worried by that French television company. That's the ace of spades in our pack of cards. You will get a decent pension, I'm sure of that, or at least a large loyalty bonus or whatever they call it. A real bonus! You will be able to hold your head up when you drink with the bankers at the Vintry." And she winked conspiratorially. "Aubrey, you are no one's fool, don't even think it. I'm secretly very proud of you. And at St Mary Abchurch, I'm even rather proud to be known as Mrs Vicar."

Chapter 12

December

Matters progressed quickly in December. The diocese had the secret agreement with a large property company to honour and couldn't afford to waste time unnecessarily. The talks had been protracted over several months already and there was now a real worry in the Bishop's Office that they would fall through. So many interested parties also had to be contacted in December, and that would mean lengthy discussions, and walks around the various buildings involved, all whilst trying to ensure that the press did not start to become interested. And December is always a busy month for all ecclesiastical authorities and tempers were starting visibly to fray in the diocese. In this complex mix, the Vicar of Abchurch was nothing more than a minor irritant which might easily be settled without delay.

"They will throw money Abchurch's way," John had assured Adrian, tapping his pocket as he made this forecast.

And sure enough, at the beginning of the month, soon after the interview with Andrew Grist, Aubrey did receive a revised pension and bonus letter. And the diocese had indeed found a way to be more generous. The bonus in particular took the vicar by surprise.

"Look at this, my dear," he said. "Just look at that amount! Do you think it's a mistake? Perhaps I should ring the area dean."

"That's no mistake," smiled Joan, looking over his shoulder. "You are being silenced with kindness. At the deanery, I would often see Daddy sort out trouble this way. Throw money at a problem. The age-old answer to anything which can't be properly managed satisfactorily some other way. Daddy's motto when faced with such an issue was 'Promote him or pay him'. I've often heard him mutter some such thing! But let's be clear," she continued in reflective mood as Aubrey still looked perplexed. "You are being told to retire three years before you legally have to do so. That's worth a monetary value. And looking at this letter, they clearly want us to move out of here by Christmas. Time is apparently vital to them. Well, speed also has a monetary value to us as well as to them. So I guess that means that we've lots to do very quickly before the end of the year. No, Aubrey, that bonus was not a mistake. Definitely no need for you to phone the area dean.

"Actually, my dear, thinking about it, your letter contains many sadnesses," she mused on reading it a second time. "And not just about you personally. I notice for instance that they don't mention a replacement vicar or even a period of interregnum. They don't even try to disguise their deceit. No, it's true, shutting St Mary's was clearly on the bishop's agenda." she sighed. "You were right. After all these centuries of Protestant worship, you, Aubrey, will be the last Vicar of St Mary Abchurch. Think of that. Some of these monuments around us must sense what is happening and be very sad indeed. Are we the last people in the City of London or indeed the country to value our rich and important history! Does this magnificent architecture mean nothing to anyone anymore? Yes, Aubrey, I've come around to your way of thinking about this place. It does have a magic of its own. And I do feel that we are connected to the generations which have gone before. Sir Christopher Wren did build wisely and well. And by the way, being practical if the diocese wants us out quickly, well, now that we have this letter there's no reason to delay anything. No reason to hang around even until the new year. We don't have to rely on the Church for our living accommodation. Perhaps you can make an announcement during the bell blessing service."

Aubrey was about to reply but thought better of it and stayed silent. He suddenly felt very sad and depressed, the tenor of Joan's remarks weighing heavily upon him. That same afternoon he decided to put the finishing touches to his carol service which as planned on this occasion, of course, would incorporate the baptism of the recast Abchurch bell.

"Joan," he said, "I had been considering to ask the area dean to come along to perform the actual blessing of the bell. In fact, it was on my mind when I met him at the end of November. But the opportunity didn't arise and my thoughts were on other things. Now mulling over the matter and all that has happened, I don't think I will bother. I'm an ordained minister in the Church of England and as such can perform the task quite legitimately."

"Excellent!" exclaimed Joan loudly. "I fully approve. At last you are becoming the man I wanted to marry!"

The carol service did indeed take place in the second week of December. Aubrey had advertised it at his various church services over the previous weeks and Joan had arranged to print hand bills which she distributed to the many business premises in the lanes and streets around about.

"I like carol services, of course," Aubrey had laughed to her as he put on his newly pressed black cassock, Old Salisbury style long white surplice and black stole. "But I can quite understand why some of my fellow clergy get a little bored with the same hymns and tunes year after year. I always feel it's a shame we don't have more of a tradition of an annual Advent carol service. Advent hymns have some of the best music and words in Hymns Ancient and Modern in my opinion."

"Just get on with it, Aubrey," said Joan impatiently. "The congregation values the tradition and rhythm of a carol service. It fits with this cold dark period of wintertime. And remember, this year, you do get to bless the bell. That at least will create an unusual and memorable interlude in the occasion. By the way," she continued, "that reminds me, the Whitechapel Foundry people asked me to tell you that they can hang the bell back up in the tower by the end of this week. So the parish should hear the sound of the Abchurch bell being rung, pealing out over Cannon Street and all the lanes around about before we actually say goodbye. I just hope after all this effort that people will turn up for the blessing."

The carol service was held on the tenth of the month at three o'clock. The bitterly cold day was already starting to look dark even at that hour. But in spite of the time and the frigid weather, there was no need to have been concerned about the size of the congregation. Rumours concerning the untimely end of Aubrey's ministry were already circulating throughout this part of the City. And it was as though the locals from businesses, pubs and cafes as well as people from the various regular services just had to be there to say thank you for all the couple had done.

"My goodness," whispered Aubrey to Joan as he welcomed yet another parishioner. "Wherever shall we put them all? I thought the wedding service was busy but this is something else. Help me set chairs upstairs in the balcony and in the vestry as an overflow. I wonder what the government Health and Safety officials will say. We really aren't supposed to pack people in like this!"

"They won't get the chance to comment, Aubrey. Even the police have turned up, look."

Joan smiled at two constables who were regular attendees at the Sunday Matins Service, and at the lady from the Commonwealth War Graves Commission who had brought a wreath to the Remembrance Service and had decided to return now with her niece and nephew.

People were pressed closely in the wooden pews and on the side pews which faced forward into the main body of the church. Luckily Joan had arranged to print an extra supply of service booklets which meant that just about everyone could have a copy as a memento. The title page proclaimed boldly;

'A Carol Service at the Church of St Mary Abchurch at which the recast ancient church bell will be blessed by the Vicar, Revd Aubrey Braithwaite'

The whole place spoke of a warm inner charm as outside the light quickly faded and inside the coloured lights arranged on the Christmas tree and throughout the nave, sanctuary, pulpit, font and window ledges sparkled brighter and brighter. A large nativity set donated by the coffee vendor and now set up near the altar had been specially lit to beautiful effect with many small artificial candles. A Union Jack which had been given to the church by the British Legion at the Remembrance service now hung proudly on the south wall. Abchurch was doing Aubrey and Joan very proud indeed.

"I think it's nearly three o'clock, my dear," whispered Aubrey as he indicated to his wife that she should take her place with the choir before they processed from the vestry to their position near the altar at the front of the building. "Isn't this just spectacular! Aren't people warm and kind and aren't I so lucky to have had the support of the best wife in the country for so many years." He squeezed her arm playfully.

"Oh, Aubrey," said Joan who, feeling herself choking back a tear, said no more.

The vicar nodded to Bob and the organist started the occasion with the carol, 'Once in Royal David's City.' When the music rang out, the whole congregation rose up to its feet and the choir processed slowly to their places in the choir stalls near the altar, followed, of course, by a very proud church minister.

The service was one of the happiest of the year. Everyone seemed to smile. The organist played his best. Carols and lessons tumbled one after another as the familiar words from the gospels of St Luke and St John as written in the King James Bible were spoken by volunteers from the body of the church. The whole congregation listened intently as if this was the first occasion of hearing even though the words and phrases were so familiar to them all. The vicar's short sermon was marked with similar attention and then came the climax, the moment for the blessing of the bell.

The foundry men had used various chains and pulleys to manoeuvre the bell onto wooden pallets placed centrally in the main aisle. Aubrey now walked around it and explained to the congregation that although he had been in the Church of England for so many years, he had never actually baptised a bell before so they would have to understand and be forgiving if he didn't do it quite right. Everyone grinned. Aubrey put his hand up over the bell in blessing and recited a few prayers which he had decided were appropriate for such an occasion. He also decided that in the Protestant tradition it should have the baptism name of the church, St Mary, even though he had no idea what previous generations had called it. So St Mary it was. And after this, the whole congregation rose to its feet to sing the national anthem.

The vicar pronounced a last blessing. The choir slowly processed to the back of the church to the words of the hymn 'Hark the Herald Angels Sing' and the congregation, happy and now cheerfully clutching service booklets eventually followed them and slowly dispersed noisily into the dark evening.

It was all over, really finished.

Later as she collected a few discarded service booklets and straightened the pews, Joan remonstrated with Aubrey.

"You didn't mention that we were leaving at Christmas," she said. "Several people questioned me about the rumours. I didn't know what to say. I just said you would probably tell the congregation on Sunday or issue a letter."

"Yes," apologised Aubrey. "I had intended to finish off my sermon with a short statement but somehow I just couldn't do it. We were all enjoying the occasion so much and so many people were singing so loudly that I just thought that a statement about closing the church would leave us all feeling rather dejected and flat. They tell you on those clerical courses which I hate so much that timing is everything! I wanted people to look back with pleasure at a very special event. It was about celebrating Christ's birth and baptising the bell. It wasn't about me."

At the end of the week, the engineers from the Whitechapel Foundry arrived as promised and they levered the bell by a complex arrangement of ropes and chains high up into the tower where it was fixed secure. Aubrey was then invited to be the first person to ring it.

"No, no, just a minute," he laughed. "The evening newspaper is here so I have to look the part. Let me put on my cassock and surplice. I can't look as though I just stepped in from the street. After all these years, I'm getting conscious of my public image!"

The bell was finally rung and pictures were taken for the London papers. Aubrey tolled the refreshed St Mary's bell for a full 15 minutes. The drinkers from the Vintry came in quite excitedly to watch and the coffee cart suddenly had a spurt in sales of flat white coffee. A clergyman from nearby St Stephen Walbrook also popped by to show his approval. And in spite of the undoubted physical effort of pulling on the bell rope for a protracted period, Aubrey beamed with sheer pleasure. He was just so happy that the recasting of the bell had been achieved.

"Joan, please don't think I'm silly but I know that St Paul's Cathedral can hear our bell. St Paul's knows that his Abchurch daughter is alive and healthy. He will be so relieved. The cathedral will have a very special Christmas indeed."

Joan laughed.

"You really are an old sentimentalist, Aubrey. But how can I argue? You might indeed be right. Although I should point out that St Paul's will need good ears to hear anything over the din of the evening traffic on Cannon St."

By the twentieth of the month, Aubrey and Joan were ready to leave. They had no worries about their living accommodation, of course, as Joan's legacy, not the Church of England, had provided that. Their house was not tied to Aubrey's employment. The various congregations were eventually given the news of their somewhat hurried retirement. Addresses were exchanged and promises made to keep in touch. The wedding couple brought a few expensive bottles of French wine to help Mr and Mrs Vicar celebrate Christmas in the 'appropriate way' as they said. Many from the Vintry and various offices around brought farewell cards and little festive gifts. The City Police dropped by with an expensive food hamper from a large London department store and an enormous Christmas card signed by dozens of officers from the force, thanking Aubrey for all he had done for them.

But in spite of all this exuberance, there was no disguising the sudden sadness of the mood, coming so soon after the carol service and the rehanging of the bell. The choir and organist in particular were inconsolable.

"It's all so sudden that's what I can't understand," said Bob. "Working for you two has been a dream. Made me really believe in Christ if I can be candid. Your sermons have moved me to think through some of the hidden bits of my life. I will miss both of you more than I can possibly say."

Aubrey smiled and thanked him for his kind words and for all he had achieved in bringing such good quality music to the church.

"An organist makes a church, Bob. And you have been ideal. Better than I might have expected. The services have come alive with your music and I notice that many, many people often sit outside the church just to listen to the organ when you play it. Thank you, Bob. And if you ever need a reference, please just let me know."

And then the actual moment came to leave. Joan and Aubrey collected their belongings and a large old Book of Common Prayer which the choir had bought as a memento. They switched off the lights and then arm in arm they shut the church door, turned the key in the lock and walked down the steps.

"No nasty thoughts, Aubrey," cautioned Joan. "It's all part of life. Many others endure much worse than us."

"I don't think I could think a nasty thought," murmured Aubrey, "about anyone or anything."

"No. I don't believe you could, my love," said Joan, smiling.

And with one last backward glance at the now dark windows of St Mary Abchurch, the couple were gone.

On New Year's Eve, a small group of tourists was being herded quickly into Abchurch Square by an experienced city guide. It was very cold now and he didn't want them dawdling. The atmosphere was raw and unusually for this part of London snow had been forecast for later that day. The tourists though were hardy but still wrapped up warmly, bedecked with colourful scarves flapping around their chins. The guide stopped.

"Now over here," he said, "we have St Mary Abchurch. This is one of the finest churches built after the 1666 Great Fire of London by the famous architect, Sir Christopher Wren. But as you can see, there is a notice stapled to the main door over there. It's from the bishop's office which just says the place is shut until further notice. I really don't know what to say more," he paused thoughtfully. "Rather embarrassingly, there are even rumours that it might be sold or pulled down."

"Surely not," said one astonished American visitor. "I'm sure we Americans would buy it if you Brits don't appreciate it! We bought London Bridge I seem to remember."

One or two of the group laughed.

"Well," continued the guide, "only a few months ago, no actually up to just a few weeks ago, this was one of the most vibrant churches in the City of London. A lovely vicar and his wife used to look after it and they were always very welcoming to guides like myself. But suddenly, everything changed. Almost overnight, quite literally, in fact. There was some sort of scandal, I think. I don't know the details but the vicar and his wife left in a hurry, forced retirement I suppose, and the place is now locked and as you can see looking very forlorn. It really should be loved again and opened up. I had wanted to take you inside," he continued, "to see its magnificent dome, the beautifully carved reredos with wooden fruit by Grinling Gibbons no less, its two sword rests, glorious pulpit and covered font. But it is not to be. The latest edition of my modest guide book does have most of the pictures you might like but I have to admit, it is not the same as seeing the real thing."

He held up a copy of his guidebook to show them.

"We have a couple or more churches to see before lunch so if you want to take pictures, do please be quick. I think we shall be having some snow soon," he said looking up at the sky. "Please be careful not to go near those syringes which I see have been dumped near the main door. There used to be a coffee cart in this square but even that's suddenly vanished," he added sadly as an afterthought. "A cup of hot coffee would have been very welcome."

A young member of the group suddenly ran up, laughing.

"Hey, look what I've found," he exclaimed, "it looks like a model of the dome of St Paul's Cathedral. Just dumped behind that bench."

"Put it down," exclaimed his mother. "It's broken and dirty."

Several members of the group took 'selfies' and images of the church windows and tower. The guide stamping his feet against the cold then collected everyone together and led them off quickly down Sherborne Lane.